TRUTH OR DARE

AND OTHER STORIES

NADIA KABIR BARB

RENARD PRESS

RENARD PRESS LTD

124 City Road
London EC1V 2NX
United Kingdom
info@renardpress.com
020 8050 2928

www.renardpress.com

ISBN: 978-1-80447-058-9

9 8 7 6 5 4 3 2 1

CONTENTS

TRUTH OR DARE

AND OTHER STORIES

FOR AMMA

CAN YOU SEE ME?

The chicken sandwich looked just as unappealing as it had done when the lady in the black-and-grey chequered coat had given it to him in front of the bus stop. The lettuce had that wilted 'I've seen better days' appearance, and Alex didn't much like raw tomatoes – all they did was sabotage the sandwich by making the bread soggy. A prawn one with lots of mayonnaise would be nice for a change – or even better, a tasty roast-beef sandwich with a dollop of mustard. What he wouldn't do for a hot meal right now! Sadly, wishes didn't fill bellies.

Not that he wasn't grateful for the food people gave him; it was just that they always seemed to opt for variations of chicken sandwiches. Was there some unwritten code out there that said being homeless meant you loved chicken?

The sandwich was rejected for the apple juice she had given him. He opened the bottle and took a long gulp. It had come as a meal deal with a packet of salt-and-vinegar crisps which he was saving for later. He wished he hadn't opened the sandwich, as he could have eaten it when he was really hungry. He hoped it would keep till then.

At this time of night the bridge was usually quiet, and he liked sitting and gazing out on to the water. It was peaceful. There was something mesmerising about the London skyline reflected on the Thames – the lights shimmering like fallen stars. It took his mind off having to worry about when he was going to get his next meal or where he was going to end up sleeping.

Two men stumbled past him, talking and laughing loudly. He could hear them swearing at each other as they walked past. They barely looked at him. But he was used to that. His mate Jack, who had lived on the streets for more than a decade, liked to joke that they were invisible – it was their superpower. Unlike Alex, Jack was prone to sudden fits of anger, and sometimes, as if to prove a point, he would shout, 'Can you see me?' at passers-by when they refused to make eye contact with him. More often than not it had the opposite of the desired effect.

Click, click, click – the familiar sound of heels on the pavement. He turned his head to get a better look, and saw a woman walking towards him. Maybe he could scrounge some money off her for a cup of tea.

The woman stopped a little further down the bridge and stood perfectly still. The moon was almost full, and it bathed her in its pale silvery light, rendering her as a slender, ghostlike figure gazing across the river. It was strange for someone to stop and take in the sights, especially this late – usually people hurried by with their heads down, tapping away on their mobiles. A few moments later, she started walking again. She didn't appear to have noticed him sitting a few metres away.

Alex surveyed her with curiosity as she stopped once again and stared out on to the water, immersed in her own thoughts. He watched, open-mouthed, as she put her bag on the ground and bent down to take her shoes off – there was no accounting for people's eccentricities. When she stood up her face was visible, and the light from the lamp made her appear ghoulish. It didn't help that she had black smudges around her eyes. She looked as if she had been crying.

It was only when she climbed on to the railing that Alex realised with growing dismay and a sense of panic what she was about to do – enjoying the view was definitely not her intention. For a moment he thought of slipping away and disappearing into the night. She probably wouldn't have realised he'd been sitting there in the first place. But instead he got up, the chicken sandwich falling to the ground. He tried to be as quiet as possible and slowly made his way up to her.

He wasn't sure what he was going to do once he reached her. He looked around hopefully, but there was nobody else on the bridge. The two men had disappeared into the night. Where were the nine million Londoners when you needed them? He really wasn't equipped to deal with this.

'Hey, lady, I wouldn't do that if I were you!' he called. His voice sounded high-pitched, and he winced at its shrillness. His heart was pounding.

The woman turned her head sharply at Alex's sudden appearance and her foot slipped, throwing her off balance. His hand shot out instinctively, but she grabbed on to the lamp post. The last thing he wanted was for her to fall in because of him. He cleared his throat.

'I really wouldn't do that if I were you,' he repeated. He sounded more like himself this time.

9

The woman frowned as she peered down at him. She reminded him of a sad panda. Her eyes were sunken, and there was a lost look in them – a look which was familiar to Alex.

'It's filthy down there,' he said, pointing at the murky water. 'Full of piss and shit.'

Her frown deepened.

'I'd know, cos I've pissed in it – a couple of times,' he said, trailing off. He wasn't sure why he had felt the need to fabricate this additional piece of information.

'Please leave me alone,' she said, her voice barely audible.

Alex shrugged. 'I can't do that.'

'Just go away!' She looked out on to the water, as if willing him to disappear.

'I'm not goin' anywhere. I was here before you, so you should leave,' he said, blurting out whatever came into his mind. He noticed she was still holding on to the lamp post.

'Listen, lady, if you were to go and jump,' he gestured to the river, 'I'd have to try and save you. And I can't swim. Well, I can, but I'm a bit rubbish… I'd probably drown and… and the water's really cold, too.' His voice sounded pleading at this point. For a moment he contemplated whether he would actually jump in after her if she did decide to throw herself in. He hoped he wouldn't have to find out.

She didn't say anything. She just stood there, balanced precariously, staring into the water.

'I'll have to report it to the police, and then they're gonna think I had something to do with it, and they'll haul me in and question me and God knows what else… that's not right, is it?' he rambled, hoping that if he kept talking someone else might pass by and help. No such luck. There was the option of running to the main road and asking a passer-by for help, but in the mean time he was worried she might jump.

Suddenly her face crumpled and she started crying. Alex was at a loss as to what to do. They stayed where they were for what felt like a long time. Her tears rolled down her face and on to her clothes. He stood there trying not to make any sudden movements.

'Come on down,' he said. 'Maybe you can call someone to come and get you?'

The crying turned into great big sobs. Alex wished he'd walked away when he had the chance.

'Wha'ever it is, it's not worth it. Please, just get off there.'

Another few minutes went by. She remained stationary, standing on the railing, holding on to the lamp post.

'Please!' Alex held out his hand. He was sweating despite the cold. Living on the streets wasn't easy, but at least he only had to look out for himself. Right now, someone else's life was in his hands. It was an overwhelming responsibility.

He couldn't say whether it was a few seconds or minutes that they both stood staring at each other, and he realised he had never been so scared in his life.

Then she reached out, took his hand and clambered off the railing. Alex's shoulders sagged with relief, and he wiped his sweaty hands on his oversized jacket. Everything looked oversized on him.

The woman slumped on to the ground and wiped her face with the sleeve of her coat. It left a black mark on the tan-coloured fabric. He wondered whether he should pat her shoulder, but was worried about how she might react. He seated himself on the ground beside her, but not close enough to frighten her.

11

They sat quietly for a while. All she did was stare at the pavement and twirl the ring on her finger. Round and round. It was almost hypnotic watching her. She wasn't sobbing any more, but the tears were trickling down her cheeks in black rivulets and she kept biting her lower lip.

Alex suddenly felt an odd sensation in the pit of his stomach and wondered whether it was hunger or relief. 'I've got a chicken sandwich if you're hungry…?' he said, remembering too late that it had fallen on the ground.

She glanced at him and shook her head, which was a relief, as he had a vision of himself saying, 'Hey, here ya go – it's freshly scraped off the ground!'

He reached into his pocket and fetched out a small bottle of whisky. He had found it on a wall near a pub, and had kept it for when things got a bit rough. This was unquestionably the time for a swig or two or three. The liquid was fiery as it slid down his throat, and he sent up a silent thank-you to whoever had left it on the wall. He offered it to the woman. She wrinkled her nose distastefully at the bottle, vigorously shaking her head, her long black hair swinging from side to side.

'Suit yourself,' he said, taking another gulp. 'I'm Alex,' he added.

'Nina,' she responded, her gaze fixed on the ground.

Silence.

Alex felt the warmth of the whisky spreading through him. It was a good feeling.

'Why are you out here?' she asked after a while.

The question caught him off guard and he paused for a moment before saying, 'Just enjoyin' the view.' This was accompanied by a forced laugh. He wasn't sure how else to answer.

She ignored his attempt at humour. 'Shouldn't you be at a shelter or something?'

'Nah,' he said, 'don't like 'em.'

Nina turned to face him, a furrow marring the smoothness of her forehead.

'Better out here than in there with the druggies,' he went on. 'You gotta be careful, cos they pinch things when you're sleeping. They can get a bit rough. When they're high you don't wanna be around. It's better off out here.'

'Oh, I didn't realise...' she said, and pulled up her legs, resting her chin on her knees.

'It's not all bad,' Alex said. 'I just don't like 'em much.'

Silence.

Apart from during the summer, the bridge was never an ideal place to sleep, but Alex liked being by himself, and a few hours of quiet contemplation every now and then made a difference. The nights were already getting colder, and he and Jack would have to try and find shelter in the doorway of one of the bigger shops. At least that would give them a bit of cover from the wind and the rain – although these days, some of the stores had taken to installing retractable metal posts which came out at night to stop people like him sleeping in their doorway. 'Fucking antisocial,' was Jack's take on it.

Alex picked at a piece of thread that was coming loose from his jacket and sat quietly next to Nina. The jacket had been given to him by the owner of an antique shop. The elderly gentleman was a regular at the Tesco Alex used to sit in front of when he was trying to sell copies of *The Big Issue*. One day the owner had suggested Alex come to his shop (one which, in Alex's opinion, looked like it was full of junk) so that he could give him an old jacket and some gloves. The jacket had been a little too big for him, but it was in good condition and, more importantly, warm. He had accepted it gratefully, along with the bowl of soup and hunk of bread he had been offered. The owner had died soon after, and the antique shop had become a hairdressing salon.

'So, what's your story?' asked Alex, not looking at Nina. He wasn't sure he really wanted to know, but he felt like he had to say something. The silence was making him uncomfortable.

'My husband left me…' she said, with a hint of a tremor in her voice, making it crack.

It was Alex's turn to frown. So some bloke had dumped her and she was thinking of ending it all.

'Sorry 'bout that,' he said. He hoped she wasn't going to cry again.

'You must think I'm stupid,' she said, looking down.

He stopped himself from nodding in agreement.

'We'd been married for ten years and he leaves me for another woman. Just like that. The worst thing is I was pregnant when he told me. We'd been trying for years to have a baby and he tells me when I'm pregnant. Who does that?' Her voice was shaking, the sadness replaced by anger.

He wished she would stop talking. He didn't need to know all this. It wasn't his business.

She echoed his thoughts. 'I don't know why I'm even telling you.'

Silence.

'I lost the baby. I think he was relieved when I told him.'

'Shit man, that's harsh,' was all Alex could say. He was totally out of his depth.

'The divorce went through today… lost my husband, lost my baby, didn't know what else to do. Sat in the car for

14

hours, then drove here.' There was a flash of anger but it was fleeting. 'He proposed to me here – right here,' she said, pointing to a spot near where they were sitting.

More silence.

'Don't you wanna call your family?' Alex asked cautiously. The last time he had mentioned calling someone it had brought on a deluge of tears.

She shook her head again.

He thought it wise to refrain from asking why not.

'What about you?' she asked. 'You didn't run away or anything, did you?'

'Nah.'

She looked at him enquiringly.

'My mum kicked me outta the house when she moved in with her new boyfriend. Didn't have anywhere to go, so started sleeping on the streets.' He couldn't remember the last time he had been honest about anything with anyone – even with Jack. Theirs was not a sharing-of-life-stories kind of relationship. They just kept an eye on each other and made sure no one stole their belongings or tried harassing them.

It was a strange feeling telling her about his mum. The pity in Nina's eyes reminded him why he didn't like talking to people about himself – not that there were many people who asked, or cared.

'It's not so bad,' he lied.

'How old were you?'

Alex took another swig from the bottle. 'Seventeen when they decided to kick me out. My mum gave me fifty quid and told me to stand on my own two feet and stop being a waste of space. Been two years now, and I'm better off without 'em.'

'You look so young.'

Alex heard that quite frequently. His inability to grow any substantial amount of facial hair and his slight frame made him seem younger than he was.

'What about your dad?'

'He died when I was a kid. Don't remember much about him.'

'I'm sorry to hear that.'

More silence.

'Well, we're quite the pair, aren't we?' said Nina, the ghost of a smile playing on her lips.

'Yup. We should go in for a "whose life is more screwed up" competition. I think I'd win,' said Alex, letting out a deep sigh.

'I really am sorry,' said Nina. This time the sadness seemed to encompass them both. 'No one should have to live out here.'

'It's all right. You get used to it after a while.' He smiled a tired smile – one that didn't reach his eyes. 'You know, you remind me of an Indian presenter on telly. She was on a show called *East meets West.*' He tried to recall the name of the presenter. Each episode was filmed in a different country around the world, with the host showcasing the culture and cuisine of the various places. He'd never been anywhere interesting in his life, unless Brighton could be considered exotic, and for an hour he had felt like he was part of their journey.

'Bangladeshi, not Indian,' she said, almost mechanically.

'You've seen it too?' he said. 'It was a good show. Shame they stopped it.' He still couldn't remember the name of the presenter. Mandy something. 'I didn't know she was Bangladeshi. My dad was from there.'

This time it was Nina's turn to look at him with interest. 'You're Bangladeshi?'

'Well, my dad was,' he said. 'Worked in a restaurant here, met my mum and ended up marryin' her. She's English. They had me and then he died.'

'Don't you have any relatives you could have stayed with? You know, on your dad's side?'

'I don't think he had any here. His family disowned him when he married Mum, so – no.'

He heard a noise and saw a couple walking towards them, holding hands. They passed Alex and Nina. The woman whispered something to the man and he glanced back at them, but kept on walking. They must have looked incongruous sitting on the pavement. He felt a poke in his arm and saw that Nina was pointing at the bottle of whisky. He passed it to her. She smiled at him, and it changed her face completely. She was a nice-looking woman. He wondered how old she was. Maybe in her thirties.

'Getting a bit chilly,' she said, wiping the mouth of the bottle and taking a sip. It made her cough and she grimaced. She didn't look like the whisky-drinking type.

Alex took out a well-worn beanie from his pocket and offered it to her.

'No, thanks,' she said, smiling at him, flashing a row of perfect white teeth. He couldn't remember the last time he'd been to a dentist.

He pulled the woollen hat over his mop of dark, curly hair. The weather had turned over the last few days and it was starting to get cold.

'So you have no relatives on your dad's side, but couldn't you have stayed with your mum's relatives – or friends – while

17

you found your feet, instead of... well, here?' Nina gestured with her hands to their surroundings. She looked concerned.

'I don't think my mum ever really wanted me, so she dumped me with my gran after my dad died. I think I was four. Lived with her till I was sixteen. When she died I had to go back to my mum. Stayed with her till a boyfriend came along.'

A few of his friends had let him crash on their couch for a while, but it had only been temporary, and before too long the offers had stopped coming. The fifty quid hadn't lasted very long. His first night on the streets, he had sat on a bench outside King's Cross station waiting for the morning to arrive. He had never realised how long a night could be.

The best thing that had ever happened to Alex was being sent to live with his gran. She had been the only one in his life to truly care about him, and made him feel as if he actually mattered. Though money had been tight and he had wanted to drop out of school and get a job to help pay the bills, she had made him stay on to finish his GCSEs. As far as his gran was concerned, an education was something no one could take away from you. So he'd studied hard and done well at school. But that was then. Her death had created a hole somewhere deep in his chest. It was a void he never managed to fill.

'I'm so sorry,' said Nina. 'It's so unfair that someone like your mum gets to have a kid who she doesn't even want – and here I am, desperately wanting one.'

'Life's a bitch!' said Alex.

'Indeed it is. Talking about bitches, did I mention I introduced my husband to the woman he's run off with? An ex-colleague of mine.' The anger was back in Nina's voice, but sitting there, hunched on the ground, she just looked vulnerable, and in pain.

'Well, one day a bloke pissed on me when I was asleep, and another time they set my sleeping bag on fire,' Alex said, grinning at Nina. She looked genuinely horrified.

Was the presenter called Marina Shah? It was going to bother him until he remembered it.

'You know, I didn't come here to… but then I…' Nina said, looking across the water, unable to finish.

Alex nodded gently in acknowledgement.

'What the hell was I thinking…? He's not even worth it,' she said.

Once again the silence.

Alex wasn't sure how long the two of them were sitting under the night sky looking out on to the water, both deep in their own thoughts. Only this time it was a comfortable silence.

'OK, that's it,' said Nina, decisively. For a moment Alex was worried she was about to climb the railing again, but she was reaching for her shoes. 'I think you should come home with me.'

He frowned at her. 'What? Why would I do that?'

'Have you got anywhere else you need to be, Alex? I have a flat with a spare room, and right now I could use the company. You can come back with me and have a hot meal and stay the night.'

Who in their right mind would offer to take someone like him back to their home? 'You're havin' a laugh!' he said. 'Or you're bonkers. What if I'm a serial killer or something? You can't just ask people to go back home with you. It's bloody stupid!'

19

'Well, if you are a serial killer, it saves me from jumping into the Thames – into all that piss and shit, some of which is yours, I believe.'

It was Alex's turn to smile.

'Seriously, it's the least I can do. You did kind of save my life. You'd be doing me a favour… I don't want to call my family – or anyone – yet.'

Manina Shah – that was the name. 'Manina Shah, Nina!' he burst out. 'You're her!'

Nina raised her hands in the air. 'You got me.'

'This is crazy,' Alex mumbled, feeling a little star struck. He'd spent many an hour at his gran's watching this woman on television. She used to have short hair on the show, and her face wasn't as thin – otherwise he might have recognised her.

'I only stopped working on the programme because that bastard wanted me to,' she said. 'He complained that I did too much travelling. Told me if we were going to start a family I needed to stay at home. Being a complete idiot, I never went back. Can't believe I gave up my career for him.' For a moment Nina was lost in thought, but then she snapped back to the present. 'Anyway, come on,' she said, 'let's go.'

Alex still didn't move. She couldn't seriously be asking him to go home with her.

'Look, the bed is there if you want it… and not that I mean to be rude or anything, but you could probably use a shower…'

Alex took a deep breath. The thought of sleeping in a warm bed was tantalising – and a hot shower? He hadn't had one in – well, a long time.

'I don't know if you like rice and curry, but I think I have some leftovers at home,' she said.

Curry? He definitely liked curry. 'Is it chicken curry?'

Nina looked apologetic. 'Sorry, it's beef – do you not eat beef…?'

He definitely liked beef.

'So are you coming?' she asked again.

He could almost hear his gran telling him not to look a gift horse in the mouth. He got up and walked back to where the chicken sandwich was lying, and grabbed his tattered backpack. It only had his sleeping bag in it, but at least it was his.

'Is your name really Alex?' she called, bending to pick up her bag.

'Alexander Ahmad,' he said, pulling a face. It was a name he kept to himself.

'Actually, hang on a second, Alexander Ahmad,' said Nina, climbing up on to the railing.

'Hey, what are you doing?' said Alex, aghast.

'Hang on!' She was tugging her wedding ring off her finger. She took a deep breath and threw it into the belly of the river.

He wondered how much the ring had cost. He looked down and saw the chicken sandwich splattered on the pavement. He leant down to pick it up, and, just like Nina had done, he hurled the offending object over the railing to meet its watery grave in the murky depths of the Thames.

He turned to smile at Nina. She smiled back and started to climb down.

As if in slow motion, he saw her heel catch in the metal balustrade. As she tried to yank it out, she lost her balance. Her hand reached out for the lamp post, but she was too far from it. Her body lurched forward, and her scream was one Alex would remember every time he closed his eyes. Her arms flailed wildly, then she disappeared over the side of the bridge.

Alex's heart was beating so hard he could barely breathe as he ran to the edge of the railing. He shouted her name, but there was only silence. All he could see was the reflection of the lights twinkling on the water.

INSIDE THE BIRDCAGE

The onions made her eyes water. She chopped them into small pieces, threw them into the hot oil and watched while they sizzled and popped. Tears ran down her cheeks and fell unchecked on to the folds of her sari. If anyone walked in she could blame the onions.

Shabana felt like the walls of the tiny kitchen were closing in on her, as if the room was becoming smaller with every passing moment. The ache in her chest made it hard to breathe. Four walls didn't always make a home – they could also create a prison.

Gradually the tears turned to sobs and she pressed her hand against her mouth to stop the sound escaping. Her mother always said that keeping secrets was one step away from telling lies. Ma was a wise woman.

The secret she had kept from everyone had given her more joy than she could ever have thought possible. Joy and a sense of power. The baby had been hers – all hers. She hadn't even told her husband. It had been her secret, and she had wanted to savour every moment of it. It would only have been a question of time till she could no longer hide her growing belly, and she knew that the moment her mother-in-law found out, the baby would belong to everyone else, and she would just be the vessel – a means to an end. Maybe she was being punished for her selfishness.

She could hear coughing nearby, and wiped her tears with the *anchal* of her sari. She added the remaining spices to the onions – turmeric, chilli, coriander, salt. The smell was familiar and comforting.

Shabana's mother-in-law was always there, watching, waiting for her to make a mistake – any mistake – so she could run to her son and tell him how unlucky he was to have been saddled with a *gadha* like her for a wife. Even if breakfast was ready on time, Amma would find something else to berate her about.

She would wait eagerly for the times that both Amma and Abba left the house for a few hours to visit relatives. Those were the times she felt alive – the door to her cage would open, and for the briefest of moments she felt free.

She cut up the vegetables and tossed them in the pot with the spices, then reached up to look through the plastic containers cluttering the shelf. Rokeya *chachi*, their landlord's wife, had told her that a pinch of panch phoron added to the bhaji would give it that extra flavour. She found a little left in one of the smaller pots and, heating a small frying pan with oil, added the panch phoron, waiting till she could hear the sputtering before tipping in the mix. The aroma filled the kitchen.

Karim *chacha* and Rokeya *chachi* had always treated her with kindness, and on the rare occasions when she was alone, Rokeya *chachi* would call her over to sit and watch television with her. Those fleeting moments spent watching a film, listening to the latest Hindi songs or just whiling away time talking made her feel like a person. Her kindly and overly nosey landlady appeared to know all the gossip and neighbourhood politics, and relished filling Shabana in on all the goings-on.

Shabana could hardly believe her luck the previous week when her in-laws had gone out of town for a relative's wedding. They had stayed for three days – three whole days! It felt like Eid had come early.

After finishing the washing and cooking food for the evening, she had gone over and spent an hour with Rokeya *chachi*, enjoying the drama of a soap opera unfolding on her television screen. They had been munching away on some homemade samosas while discussing where to purchase cotton saris at the best price when she realised that something was wrong. There was an ache in her belly, making her feel sick. Rokeya *chachi* readily accepted that the pain was from an upset stomach and sent Shabana home.

By the time she walked across the corridor and stumbled through the door the pain had become unbearable and she could barely stand. It had required all her strength to get to the bathroom. She had been helpless, unable to stop her body from rejecting her unborn child. After cleaning up after herself she lay in bed, crying until her tears ran out. She felt like an empty shell. Her husband had believed her when she told him that she was suffering from one of her headaches, and had left her to rest.

A week had gone by, and it was her fault that she was the only one grieving the loss of her baby. How strange that everything could change from one breath to the next.

Another cough. She looked up to see Amma sticking her head through the doorway. Her hair was scraped back into a neat little bun at the nape of her neck, and the cotton sari draped around her was starched and pressed. The first time Shabana had brought Amma a freshly starched sari she had actually smiled and patted her on the head. For a moment, Amma had forgotten that she was the daughter-in-law she never wanted. At home, Ma had taught her how to starch saris by dipping them in water saved from straining the rice and then rinsing them out – this gave them a crispness when they dried.

Looking at Amma, Shabana could see that her mother-in-law must have been quite beautiful when she was younger. These days a permanent scowl adorned her face, and her teeth were stained from the constant chewing of betel leaves.

'Don't put too much salt in the bhaji like last time. It was inedible. *Chee!*' She wrinkled her nose and shook her head. Shabana tried not to laugh as she remembered Amma polishing off every last morsel on her plate.

'*Ji*, Amma,' she responded dutifully.

'And be quick – we're all hungry. Can't wait around all day for you to serve the food.'

'*Ji*, Amma.'

She could hear her mumbling as she walked away.

Her father used to tell her that she had magic in her hands, that the food she cooked left you licking your fingers and wanting more. Here, her cooking was always wanting. She sometimes wished she did have magic in her hand – so she could make Amma disappear.

Soon the bhaji was ready, the chapatis were made and the tea was piping hot. She called her husband and in-laws for breakfast and headed over to the dining room next to the kitchen, with its small table, brown sofa and cane chair.

The room was cramped, but it was still far better than the previous place they had rented, where they had eaten their meals sat on the kitchen floor.

She served the food on to Amma and Abba's plates and then her husband's. The three of them sat at the table eating while she fanned them with a bamboo hand *pankha*. There was no ceiling fan in the room, just a table fan, which was only used when the heat was unbearable. When Amma and Abba were away, Shabana and her husband took the fan through to their bedroom to enjoy the coolness it provided, always being careful to put it back before her in-laws returned. Abba thought using the fan on a regular basis was a waste of money.

As they ate, she looked around the room, taking in the faded floral curtains and the small brass vase on the table filled with gaudy plastic flowers. The flowers made her sad.

A few months ago, they had been invited to Abba's niece Rozina's wedding ceremony. Shabana had found a stray marigold that had fallen from one of the decorations, and she picked it up and put it in her hair.

Amma had yanked the flower out roughly and thrown it back on the ground. 'Don't make a spectacle of yourself! I don't know what your parents taught you, but in this family, we don't behave in such a vulgar way. What will people say?' she had hissed at her.

When Shabana and her two sisters were children, they would make garlands from flowers they found lying around. Her favourite had always been jasmine. The three girls would pretend they were princesses with their crowns of white scented flowers. Shabana wondered how putting flowers in her hair could be considered vulgar.

When they returned home from the wedding and were finally in the privacy of their bedroom, her husband had tried to comfort her. That was the first time she realised that she loved him. He was a good man – albeit weak.

Shabana wondered what would happen if she told them about the baby. Amma would blame her for not being able to bear a child. 'Damaged goods', 'worthless' – she could almost hear her saying it. But this time Amma wouldn't be wrong; she was defective.

Always a sickly child, she had had problems breathing, and every cold would go straight to her chest. Then there were the headaches, which felt like a thousand nails being hammered into her head. Sometimes they would only get better after she had vomited up the contents of her stomach. Ma and Baba didn't even think she would survive her first year. Unfortunately for Amma, *gadhas* were stubborn creatures.

These days, all she could do was take some paracetamol and pray that the pain would subside. Abba thought it was an excuse for her to get out of doing her chores.

Life had taught her that there was no place for the old and physically weak or sick in this world. Even if Ma and Baba had never said it in as many words, she knew she was a burden to them. Frequent visits to the doctor and constant medicines for something or other didn't come cheap. Her marriage had been one where both families benefited.

Ma and Baba said it was to secure her future. She would have a husband to look after her when they were both gone. Her in-laws had agreed to the marriage on the basis that her father would guarantee a job for her husband-to-be at the office where he worked. They were also promised two mobile phones, a Seiko watch, two beds and an almirah. That was her worth to her mother and father and to her in-laws.

She leant over and gave her husband another chapati. He smelt of soap and his face was freshly shaved. There was a small cut on the side of his chin, and she wanted to reach out and touch him, to tell him how sorry she was.

The delicate aroma of the food wafted up to her nose and she realised her stomach was rumbling with hunger. When they were newly married, her husband had suggested she ate with them, but Abba said that she should eat after everyone had finished. She had hoped her husband would fight a little harder, but he had just kept quiet. These days she preferred to have her meals by herself anyway.

'Shabana, I left two files on the bed,' said her husband, briefly looking up from his food. 'Can you get them for me? I need them for work today.'

She nodded and went to fetch the files for him. The covers were hard and shiny. They looked important.

'I hope they're treating you well at work, Anwar *baba*, you're looking tired,' said Abba, gesturing to Shabana with his hand for another chapati.

'Yes, everyone is very nice,' said Anwar. 'They've given me a project to look after, and it's a big responsibility – especially as I'm still quite new compared to some of the other fellows working there.' There was a tinge of pride in his voice.

Abba smiled. 'Don't let them work you too hard or take advantage of you.'

'No, Abba, I won't, don't worry.'

'They are so lucky to have someone like you,' said Amma, in a way that Shabana felt was somehow directed at her.

29

When everyone had left the table, she cleared up and washed all the dirty pots, pans, plates and cups. She ate a chapati and some bhaji and gulped down a cup of tea. There was still sweeping and mopping to do before she got to washing the clothes.

Life had become a routine for her, looking after the household and its members, each day bleeding into the next. There was hardly anything to break the monotony.

A few months after being married, when her husband had got the new job promised by her father, he had taken her to see a Bengali film showing at their local cinema. Amma had stopped talking to him for the next few days, and Abba said it was a waste of money. It was unsurprising, really – Abba thought everything was a waste of money. They hadn't been to see a film since.

Rupa *khala*, her mother-in-law's younger sister, had let slip one time that Amma had never wanted to marry Abba. When the proposal had come, she had considered him to be a miserly young man with a lowly job. But their parents had dictated who was suitable for her. The oldest daughter of a family of seven, she had been married off as quickly as possible, and Amma had never forgiven her parents or Abba for not giving her the life she wanted.

Her ambitions for a better life seemed to have been transferred on to her son, and Shabana felt that somehow she didn't fit the image of the daughter-in-law Amma had envisaged.

Shabana gathered up the clothes for washing and realised that there was something heavy in her father-in-law's trouser pocket. She put her hand inside and pulled out his mobile phone – he must have left it there by mistake.

She looked around then slowly hid it in the folds of her sari and walked silently to her bedroom. Inside the wooden almirah was a small box of bangles. She opened the box and took out a piece of paper that was tucked into the bottom. She unfolded it with trembling hands and called the number. She wasn't usually allowed to use the phone without permission.

Her father answered. She could feel tears pricking the back of her eyes.

'Baba?'

'Shabana?' He sounded surprised. 'How are you? Is everything OK?'

'I'm fine, Baba, I just wanted to hear your voice,' she said quietly. The last thing she wanted was for Amma to catch her with the phone.

'You're sure everything is all right? You don't usually call when I'm in the office,' he said.

'How is Ma?' she asked, ignoring his question.

'Yes, she's fine – she misses you. We haven't seen you for almost a month. You should come and see her soon… your sisters ask about you too.'

'I will, Baba. Tell Moina and Rina to study properly and not to spend their time daydreaming.'

'Don't worry – both of them are working hard for their exams.'

'Baba, I should go now,' she said. She couldn't stop her voice from shaking. She wanted to tell him how much she wanted to come home, put her head on her mother's lap and let the tears out till there was nothing left. She wanted to feel her mother's hands stroking her head, to hear her voice telling her everything would be all right.

Instead she hung up and put the phone on the table in the living room. She hoped Abba would think he just left it there.

After washing her face and composing herself, she went back to her chores.

Even those few words with her father made things bearable, and the rest of the day passed uneventfully. She was relieved when night-time came and she could retire to the bedroom.

She lay down and closed her eyes. The weariness in her body seemed to have woven itself into every fibre of her being. She felt her husband reach for her, his hand brushing against her breast, and she recoiled. Almost immediately, he pulled his hand away and turned to face the other way.

The guilt rose in waves inside her. She wanted to reach out, to take his hand and place it on her belly. She wanted him to put his arms around her and take the emptiness away. Instead they lay there in the dark, back to back, silent. Soon the night enveloped them both.

* * *

The morning came too quickly and Shabana dragged herself out of bed. She could hear the azaan in the distance. The morning light washed over the streets and buildings around her, and she watched through her window as Dhaka awakened.

Friday began much the same way as any other day. The only difference was Abba and her husband were at home. She prepared breakfast and finished her daily tasks and waited for them to leave the house for their Jummah prayers before going for her bath.

She came out of the bathroom and combed her wet hair in front of the small mirror in her bedroom. She was no beauty – her eyes weren't big enough, and her complexion wasn't fair enough; 'passable in looks' was how she would describe herself. But her hair was thick and long, and she had been told that her smile was sweet. She wondered what her husband saw when he looked at her.

On Fridays Shabana was allowed to eat lunch with them. The day turned out to be a good one, with both Amma and Abba eating their food without any complaints.

After lunch she cleared away the plates and threw the fish bones in the garbage. From the kitchen she heard a knock at the door. It would probably be Karim *chacha* to see Abba.

Then she heard her father's voice. She hurried out of the kitchen to see whether she had been imagining it, but there he was, being greeted by Abba and Amma. She hung back, trying to listen in on the conversation to find out why he had come so unexpectedly, but was too impatient to wait. He was sitting on the sofa and looked up as she entered the room.

'Baba?' she asked, walking towards him, praying that her mother and sisters were well.

'Shabana, there you are. I was telling your mother and father-in-law that after your phone call yesterday I was very worried about you.'

She glanced at Amma, whose chest was heaving with anger. The look she directed at Shabana made it clear what was to follow when Baba left.

'Your Ma told me to come and make sure you're not sick… oh, and she sent some halwa for Anwar.' He passed her a little tiffin carrier.

She stood awkwardly for a moment, then put the container on the table and sat next to her father, wanting to know everything that had been happening at home. After a while,

33

she went to fetch some tea for everyone while her husband explained to her father the newest responsibility he had been given. Baba was all smiles when she returned with the tea.

The two fathers turned to discussing the recent strikes, shaking their heads and saying that it was always the common people, people like them, that suffered the most. Her mother-in-law barely said a word.

When her father finally took his leave, Shabana found it hard to say goodbye without breaking down. Her husband offered to walk with him to the bus stop, and she watched from the door as they disappeared into the crowd.

Her mother-in-law was waiting for her once the door had closed. 'After everything we do for you – what did you say to your father that he has to come running?'

'Amma, I…' she stammered, barely having chance to open her mouth before her mother-in-law's hand came down on the side of her face.

The slap took her by surprise. She raised her hand to her cheek. It felt hot. She tried desperately to hold back her tears – she didn't want to give Amma the satisfaction of seeing her cry.

'You ungrateful little wretch! What lies have you been telling your father?' Amma shouted. 'How dare you take your Abba's phone without asking? A liar and a thief!'

'I didn't!' she said.

The hand came down again.

This time she couldn't hold back the tears.

'Liar,' she hissed.

The third time the hand came down Shabana caught it in her own, holding the wrist tightly and pushing it away from her face.

'Enough!' came a stern voice from the doorway, making both women turn around.

Her husband was standing in the doorway watching them. She had never seen him look like this. The pain in his face was visible, but she could also see something else – anger. She was terrified it would be directed at her.

Her own anger was replaced with shame; mortified that he had seen her belittled and humiliated.

'Enough, Amma!' he demanded again, and walked over and put his arms around Shabana.

Amma opened her mouth to say something, but he put his hand up to silence her.

'Are you all right, Shabana?' The tenderness in his voice made her heart ache and she nodded.

He touched her cheek, his hand cool and gentle on her face. 'Go and wash your face,' he said, 'then go and put on your best sari.'

She looked at him, unable for a moment to comprehend their meaning.

'Amma, I'm taking my wife out to see a picture. I'm sure you can make some food for us for this evening.' There was a defiance in his voice she had never heard. She barely had the courage to look at Amma's face, and just stood there.

'It's all right – go and change your sari,' he said softly.

She quickly turned around and ran to the bathroom to wash her face. She rummaged around in the almirah and took out a sari she had worn on Eid – a blue sari with a pink pattern, given to her by her parents.

When she emerged from the bedroom her husband was waiting for her with a smile on his face and an expression she had been longing to see. Her mother-in-law was

35

standing in the doorway, her face contorted in anger but also tinged with what Shabana could only describe as bewilderment – that her son could speak to her in such a manner was incomprehensible to her. Shabana almost felt sorry for her. But there was a part of her that didn't care. She stepped out on to the street with her husband and was immediately engulfed by a sea of people pushing and jostling them, but she barely noticed. All she was aware of was her heart soaring.

LIVING WITH THE DEAD

I often think about death. It used to lurk in the deep recesses of my mind, but these days it pops up like a jack-in-the-box with an annoying frequency. The preoccupation has long ceased to be a fear of dying, and over time had evolved into an acceptance of the inevitable. The only questions that remain are how and when. I suppose sitting in a cemetery might have something to do with it.

I wasn't always this morbid or reclusive. Being surrounded by family and friends was something I enjoyed – or maybe I just thought I did. The desire for solitude crept up on me, and before I knew it I was spending my free time alone – perhaps because there was already enough noise inside my head. I needed peace and quiet. Time to think. Time to just be. There's something quite liberating about sitting under the great expanse of open sky with the dead as my companions. I've become acquainted with many of the residents within the walls, and my imagination has filled in the blanks: who they were, how they lived and how they died.

A couple carrying a small bunch of flowers walk past me. I shift my weight on the bench to watch where they stop. It's one of the newer graves.

I run my fingers along the peeling green paint of the wooden seat. It feels like being reacquainted with an old friend. It's been a while since I was last here. The bolt-like nail on the right-hand side is still jutting out. I reach out and touch it. The memories are as fresh as if it were yesterday. I can hear our voices in our silent surroundings.

* * *

'I think I want to be cremated,' I said quietly, while watching Leo smudge charcoal on the paper with his finger.

He looked up. 'Aren't you Muslim?'

I nodded.

'I thought you had to be buried?'

'Yes, we do. I guess if I were in Bangladesh, it might be an issue – in fact, it would definitely be an issue – but I'm here, so I hope my family will respect my wishes. Plus I'm claustrophobic. Don't like the thought of being covered by soil.' I shuddered involuntarily. 'With worms and bugs as my eternal companions? I don't think so.'

He stopped drawing and looked at me. 'I doubt you'll really care at that point – you know, with the being dead and all.' He was laughing at me.

'I didn't say it was a rational thought, just a preference.'

I rolled my eyes exaggeratedly at him, but he'd disappeared back into his sketchpad. I tried to look at his drawing, which he guarded with an uncharacteristic possessiveness.

'What about you?' I asked. 'Do you want to be buried? Cremated…?'

'Me? Don't care. When I'm dead my body's just a carcass. Makes no difference to me if I'm buried or cremated or left in a ditch to rot.' Somehow his response didn't surprise me.

'Rotting corpses in ditches aren't particularly great for the environment,' I said. 'You know, with the stench and all... plus you'd have to travel to the countryside to find a ditch. I don't think London is a ditch-rich area.'

He glanced at me and laughed. 'Point taken. OK, maybe not a ditch. But don't you think that how or when we die should be a choice? There's so much of my life I didn't get to choose. Wouldn't it be empowering to have control over our death?'

I knew he wasn't joking. We'd danced around this topic a few times in previous conversations. His father had left his mother when she had been pregnant with him. He'd never even met the man. Years of dealing with a single parent suffering from depression had left him cynical about what life had to offer. It wasn't the life he'd chosen – it had been imposed upon him. That was how he saw it.

'Choosing the time or the way you die is... well, what you're talking about is suicide. I'm not sure I agree. I think some things have to be left to chance or fate or whatever you want to call it.'

'So conventional of you, Bina.'

I didn't mind the comment so much as the accompanying look of disappointment.

He stood up suddenly. 'Let's walk.'

I got up and fell in step with him. The cemetery was empty, as usual. Over time we realised we were the only regular visitors. A world apart from the graveyard where my grandmother was buried in Dhaka. I remember the blanket of heat that engulfed me and the heady fragrance of jasmine in the air. That too was a resting place for the dead, but it hummed continuously with the sound and movement of people paying their respects to the departed. It was a place for peaceful contemplation, but not solitude. I told Leo that those who were buried there never wanted for company, with rows and rows of graves lined up next to each other.

'Aww look, Maisy Duck's had a visitor,' I said, pointing at a large gravestone with a small posy of roses. We had fallen in love with the name, and she'd become one of our favourites.

'About time. What's the point of all this?' he said, pointing to the graves surrounding us. 'Fancy headstones, elaborate epitaphs. Who the hell is even going to remember or come and visit in a few years? Ashes to ashes, dust to dust…'

'Oh, for God's sake stop being so bloody morose! I thought this place allowed you to think and meditate.'

He stopped and turned to face me. 'Are all Bangladeshi women as fierce as you?' He was smiling. 'I was going to give this to you later, but let's call it a peace offering.' He handed me the drawing he'd been working on. The woman in the sketch was undeniably me – the cheekbones, the mouth, the eyes, the hair – but it was not any me that I'd ever imagined. The lines were dark and bold, the shading deep, the angles sharp, almost exaggerated, and the contrast pronounced. It was uncharacteristic even for Leo's highly stylised sketches. And the face was beautiful. So this was how he saw me.

Before I had a chance to say anything, he bent his head and his lips covered mine. For a second I allowed myself to yield to the pressure of his mouth, and then guilt made me pull away. It felt like we were being disrespectful to the dead.

Now I wish I could return to that moment and give in to my feelings.

* * *

I first met Leo in the cemetery. We shared the view that the dead are far more accommodating and peaceful than the living. I suppose that was what brought us together in the first place: both seeking respite from the emotional cacophony that accompanies us like a constant, unwanted companion. Life with the living can be a draining experience.

At the end of spring almost two years earlier, I had agreed to attend a photography exhibition organised by Janet, an old friend from school. It was at the Dissenter's Gallery, which is adjacent to the chapel in our local cemetery. Odd place for an exhibition, I thought, but went along to show my support.

I arrived early, and because it was an unusually mild and balmy evening I wandered around the cemetery while I waited for the exhibition room to open. The first thing I noticed was the silence. It was as if even the birds had stopped chirping out of respect for the dead. I wondered why people spoke in hushed tones in a graveyard – it wasn't as if any of the inhabitants would be disturbed by the noise. The quietness seeped into my body, and I felt at peace. I sat down on a bench and looked at the assortment of tombstones. An act of homage to the people who have moved on from the people left behind.

A couple of weeks later, on my way back from work, I drove past the cemetery and, for reasons I still can't fathom, parked my car and walked in. Almost immediately a sense of tranquillity washed over me. This time I stopped to read some of the epitaphs on the headstones:

LESLIE BARKER

1967–2002

GONE BUT NOT FORGOTTEN

MARK CUMMINS
1863–1940
BELOVED HUSBAND AND FATHER

It was the inscriptions for the children that saddened me.

JENNIFER MATTHEWS
1901–1909
OUR ANGEL
WHO WATCHES OVER US FROM HEAVEN

I wondered how you could recover from the loss of a child.

I found myself returning every week to soak up the calming energy. I would walk through the grounds or sit on the green wooden bench and read.

On my fourth visit, as I sat reading, a man walked over and, without a word, parked himself on the bench. It wasn't my private property, so he didn't need to ask if he could sit down, but it irritated me. He barely even looked my way. Instead he took out a notepad and a few charcoal pencils and started scribbling. I watched from the corner of my eye. He was wearing jeans and a black T-shirt. His wavy hair was in need of a trim, as was his beard, and the black-rimmed glasses were thick and heavy on his face. He caught me staring at him, and I could feel the blood rushing to my cheeks. I tried to look nonchalant, then got up and left.

After our first encounter, every time I visited the cemetery he seemed to be sitting on the bench, pad of paper and pencils in hand. He'd encroached on my patch of peace and quiet and hijacked it. For a while I made a point of walking past or ignoring him. I'm not sure if he even noticed, but it gave me a sense of satisfaction.

It got to the stage where I expected the bearded man to be in the cemetery, and one day I decided to stake my claim. The bench was a little ahead of me, and I made my way over and sat down. He didn't look up.

'Stalking is an offence, you know?' he said.

At first I wasn't sure I'd heard correctly, but he had turned his head and was looking at me.

'What? I'm not stalk…' I trailed off. He was smiling. The man had a warped sense of humour. I gave him a perfunctory smile.

'It's a great place to think… and draw. Or read,' he said, pointing at my book.

I nodded and opened my book.

We sat in silence, and I wondered if I should introduce myself, but before I had a chance he got up.

'Enjoy,' he said, gesturing to the grounds, and walked towards the exit. Strange man.

I sat for a bit longer, finished a chapter of my novel and then took some photos of the changing sky on my phone. They turned out rather well.

I returned the following week. The man was sitting on the bench drawing. I think a part of me was secretly pleased.

'Hello again,' I said.

He gazed at me over his glasses, and for a moment I thought there was a blank look on his face. I felt like an idiot.

'Hello you. Following me again?' he said.

'Obviously,' I replied.

'Leo,' he said, offering me his hand. I reached out and shook it. There was charcoal dust on his fingertips. 'You should at least know the name of the person you're stalking.'

'And you should know the name of your alleged stalker,' I said, and smiled as I sat down on the bench. 'Bina.'

Our chance encounters became a regular occurrence, and we met other every week at the bench. We grew familiar with the names of people buried, and would often place a flower on those graves that had been long forgotten. We learnt about each other. He was a graphic designer, but liked to sketch in his spare time. He said he would never have guessed I was a school librarian. I never thought to ask what he meant.

During the winter we stopped going to the cemetery, and met instead at the local café. It wasn't the same. Too many people, too much noise. Spring saw us back at the cemetery, at our green bench. The last time I met him he gave me the portrait.

* * *

Leo died a year ago. His family buried him. Not here – in a quiet little cemetery with manicured gardens in north London. They say he didn't see the oncoming bus as he stepped off the pavement. I'm not sure I believe that. I think he chose his 'how and when'. I visited his grave a few times, but he was right. It felt like it was only his carcass lying in the casket – his essence is here. I can feel it when I walk the familiar paths flanked by the graves of people who were the silent observers in our relationship. If one can call it that.

Every day I live with the burden of 'if only'. If only I'd done something to stop him. If only I'd told him how I felt. If only I'd been enough. I wonder if he's sitting on the bench next to me now, watching me and smiling as I run my finger across the peeling green paint.

44

TRUTH OR DARE

The classroom was devoid of its usual liveliness and chatter. The stillness of the air seemed to have had a soporific effect on its occupants. Even the gecko suspended upside down on the ceiling was stationary. A thick blanket of heat engulfed the room, making it oppressive and stifling. The only sound was the scratching of chalk on blackboard. Their teacher, Mateen Sir, as he was referred to by his pupils, was writing out a mathematical equation. Once completed, he turned around and told the class to solve the problem in their exercise books, then sat down, putting his sandal-clad feet up on the rickety wooden table while observing his students. There was a gentle stirring as the boys roused themselves from their lethargy and picked up their pencils.

Raju, however, sat very still, staring intently at his unopened book. There was a black line running diagonally across the cover, and it was moving. He brought his face closer, his eyes level with the top of his desk. The little black ants were marching in a straight line, over his book and down the side of his desk. He was so fully immersed in their progress he failed to notice Mateen Sir walking up to him. It was only when the wooden part of the blackboard duster was thwacked on

45

his head that he looked up. He could feel a shower of the powdery chalk dust settle on his forehead and nose. He cried out in pain and instinctively touched the top of his head.

'Stand up!' shouted Mateen Sir.

Raju moved his chair back and stood up. He could see the boys looking up from their books.

'Are you deaf? Do you have a problem with your ears?' Sir demanded.

Raju shook his head, but knew better than to answer. Sir loved to dole out punishment to boys who talked back.

'What did I ever do to deserve a bunch of lazy buggers like you as my students?' His nasal voice sounded even higher pitched than usual. Having failed to secure a position in an office environment, Mir Mohammed Mateen had taken up teaching as a fallback option – one he regretted every day. This was conveyed to his students on a regular basis.

One of Raju's classmates, Masood, had informed them that Sir was actually possessed by a djinn. He had seen him lying on the floor of the school veranda a few months ago, shaking and writhing uncontrollably, with white foam coming out of his mouth. The other teachers had to pry his mouth open with something. Masood said he couldn't be certain what the item used had been, as his view had been obscured by the teachers. Since then the boys had been far more circumspect and respectful around Mateen Sir.

Sir was standing so close to Raju that he was accosted not only by the yellow stains on Sir's white shirt, which formed an almost circular pattern under his armpits, but also the overpowering stink of stale sweat.

Raju held his breath while he waited. He wondered what punishment he had to look forward to. Sir's favourite was

46

getting them to stand with their arms outstretched, a book on either palm. The duration corresponded with the perceived severity of the crime. Sometimes he would make them hold their ears and do squats. Sir also liked to hit the palm of their hands with a stick he kept in the corner of the room – although this punishment was painful, it was over relatively quickly.

But for once it appeared that luck was on Raju's side, and the bell signifying the end of school rang out. Within seconds everyone in the room jumped to their feet and slammed their books shut. Raju waited. Mateen Sir had to wrestle between the thought of being rid of his pupils for the day or dispensing some well-deserved punishment on one of them. He chose the former and, after rapping the duster on Raju's head one more time, let him go.

Raju picked up his book and gently tapped it on his desk. He hoped this would cause the least disruption for the ants. They landed on the wooden surface in a state of disarray, but within moments resumed their steady descent down the side of his desk. Satisfied, he packed his bag and ran to join his friends, Shojib and Tito, on their walk home.

The pavement was crowded with people, and the narrow road was heaving with bicycles, rickshaws, cars and scooters. The three boys weaved their way through the chaos – a game in itself, where they zigzagged through the people, avoided falling into the open drains on the side and jumped out of the way of oncoming traffic.

Raju left his two friends and turned into the alley leading up to his house. He was suddenly aware of his stomach reminding him that he hadn't eaten anything since he had left for school in the morning, except for a banana during tiffin time.

47

'Maaaa, I'm hungry!' he shouted, as he ran through the door. The bag was thrown carelessly on to the floor, along with his green water bottle.

His mother was in their small kitchen scrubbing some dirty pots. It felt hotter inside the room than it did under the scorching sun outside.

'What happened to you? You look like an old man,' she said, smiling at him, as she looked up. Raju remembered the chalk dust on his head, and he smiled back.

'Go and wash yourself first.'

'*Achcha*, Ma!' he said, running into the bathroom. He cast off his light-blue school shirt and navy shorts and filled the bucket with water, bathing as quickly as he could. The cool water felt good on his hot skin. The bar of soap residing on the windowsill lay unused. Ma would never know.

By the time Raju returned to the kitchen she had already put some rice, daal and fish on a plate for him. He sat down on the floor next to his mother and mixed the food together before gulping it down.

'*Hai hai!* Slow down,' said Ma. 'You'll get a stomach ache. What's the rush – do you have a train to catch?'

Raju giggled. 'I'm playing cricket with Tareq, Ma. I don't want to be late.' He licked his fingers clean. His mother passed him a glass of water, which he drank just as quickly, and stood up to wash his hands under the tap in the corner of the kitchen.

He thought it prudent not to tell her that they had decided to climb to the top of a ten-storey building that was still under construction. The workers on the site had shooed them away on a couple of occasions, saying it was dangerous, so they had planned to go when the site would be less busy – or

48

better still, empty. It was a dare they had both accepted, and neither had the intention of backing down. Raju hadn't told Tareq he was afraid of heights, but, at the age of eleven, not going through with a dare was unthinkable and tantamount to being labelled a coward – he would climb to the top even if he died trying, so firm was his resolve. He could almost see his body lying on the ground, his bones broken into a hundred pieces. If he survived the fall, his father would most certainly kill him for lying to his mother.

The schoolbag was retrieved from where he had discarded it, and after a little bit of rummaging inside, he found his recently acquired, most prized possession – a red-and-yellow striped spinning top. It was sitting hidden away, right at the bottom, nestled between his maths and geography textbooks. He wound the string around the wooden top, and with a skilful flick of his wrist sent the top twirling and dancing on the floor. When it finally came to a halt he picked up the top and stuffed it into his pocket, along with the string. Raju wanted to show Tareq his new find. He had spotted it lying near the school gates when he had arrived for school in the morning. By the end of the day, as no one had claimed the object, he felt it acceptable – obligatory, even – to take it home.

'I'm going, Ma,' he shouted on his way out, and heard her telling him to come home before dark.

The sun was still hanging high in the sky, a lone *cheel* circling above, as Raju sped off towards the construction site. He could feel the sweat trickling down his back as he made his way through the narrow alleys.

It had been a matter of pride when Tareq had befriended Raju in school from the day he had joined – an unwritten alliance had been forged between them, since their fathers worked as drivers for the same company. Raju's classmates had been envious of him finding favour with one of the older boys, especially as Tareq was one the three 'leaders' in the school. It made Raju untouchable – none of the boys would dare bully or harass him. No one wanted to get on the wrong side of Tareq or his friends.

Raju ran the last bit of the way. In his eagerness to show Tareq his spinning top, he had for a brief moment forgotten the real reason for their meeting. As the construction site came into view, he saw Tareq, his long limbs splayed out in front of him, sitting on a pile of bricks stacked just outside the corrugated metal barrier. He was so deeply absorbed in his own thoughts he didn't see his friend approaching. In fact, he didn't hear his name being called until Raju jumped on him in a playful tackle.

He pushed Raju off, causing him to stagger backwards and nearly fall on to the heap of bricks. 'Hey, why did you do that?' asked Raju reproachfully.

'You shouldn't creep up on people if you don't want to get shoved,' Tareq said, his voice unusually brusque.

Raju noticed his eyes were red and puffy. He wondered if he had been crying.

'Are we going to climb to the top or sit here like a sack of potatoes?' Raju said with false bravado. He looked up at the concrete structure looming above them. He had never been in a building as tall as this one, and he could feel his heart thumping in his chest like a tabla. It was so loud he thought Tareq might hear. There were no walls or rooms yet, just the bare bones of the building, with metal rods jutting out everywhere. The first few floors had concrete stairs leading up, but the higher floors were accessible only by means of some makeshift bamboo ladders.

Tareq gazed up and frowned. 'We can't – look – there are some workers up there,' he said, pointing to one of the higher floors. 'They'll just chase us off. We'll have to come back another time.' He didn't sound particularly sad by the turn of events.

So he wasn't going to die today after all, thought Raju with relief. The sudden respite from impending death made him want to pee. He asked Tareq to wait while he unzipped his shorts and relieved himself by the side of the road. With luck, Tareq would forget their dare in time.

He remembered he had his spinning top in his pocket, and took it out to show his companion. Tareq placed it in his hand, scrutinising the top with the eyes of a connoisseur. He nodded in admiration. They moved away from the construction site and found an even patch of ground, where Raju demonstrated his skill with another flick of his wrist. It went spinning on the dusty ground, leaving circular tracks with its metal pin. Then Tareq showed Raju how to get the top off the ground on to his palm without disrupting its motion. As Raju looked at the wooden object going round and round, he noticed that there was a red welt around Tareq's wrist, and there was a bruise further up his arm.

He looked at his friend. 'Did he beat you again?'

Tareq didn't look at Raju but nodded. He kept his eyes firmly on the spinning top, which was now coming to the end of its dizzying cycle.

On more than one occasion Tareq had been on the receiving end of his father's anger – a man known for his temper and foul mouth. Tareq had frequently shown up in school with a cut lip or bruises on his arms or legs. No one had asked how he had injured himself – not even the teachers. Raju had, in his childish innocence, been persistent, and after the initial few rebuffs had been sworn to secrecy by Tareq.

Raju knew better than to ask any more questions, and they played on the side of the road with the spinning top, making it whirl and twirl to their whim. Afterwards they ran down the street chasing each other, laughing at the pedestrians who shouted and cursed at them for colliding into them. They stopped by Alamgir's sweet shop, gazing with hungry eyes at the wondrous selection of sweets on offer.

Tareq rummaged in his pocket and took out a dirty ten-taka note. 'I found it on the street,' he said, waving the note in the air, and entered the shop with a swagger. He returned with two juicy *roshogollas*. They bit into the sweets, unperturbed by the sweet syrup running down their hands. They devoured them quickly, licking their hands dry, before continuing their chase. Soon the sky turned from blue to orange as the sun made its descent for the day. The call to Maghrib prayers was a sign it was time for Raju to head home. Reluctantly the boys parted ways.

'See you in school tomorrow,' Raju shouted to Tareq, but his friend had already disappeared into the crowd.

The following morning Raju walked to school by himself. His mother had insisted on putting oil in his hair before allowing him to leave the house, which had resulted in him missing both Shojib and Tito. Going by himself wasn't much fun. He arrived just in time for the morning bell, running into the classroom before the teacher came to take the roll call. From the moment he entered the room, he knew something was wrong. The boys fell silent and whispered to each other, all the while watching him with curious eyes.

'Hey, what are you staring at? Have I got two heads?' Raju said to the class.

Shojib came forward. 'Haven't you heard?' he asked breathlessly, his face brimming with excitement.

'Heard what?'

'*Aai hai*, about Tareq?'

Raju could feel a tightness in his chest. 'What's happened to Tareq?'

Shojib looked at the others and then said in a lowered voice, 'He beat his father to a pulp. The police have taken him to the local police station and locked him up. I heard his father hit his mother so hard he cracked her skull. Tareq tried to stop him.'

Raju listened, wanting to disbelieve Shojib's story but knowing it to be true.

'His father hit Tareq with an iron rod,' Tito interjected. 'Tareq grabbed it and started hitting his father back till he was almost dead.' There was a certain amount of relish in his voice as he recounted this piece of information.

'They took his father to the hospital – if he dies it'll be a murder case!' said Shojib, his eyes so wide they looked as if they might pop out of his head.

Raju looked at the boys, their young faces watching him intently, waiting for his reaction. Raju said nothing. He slowly picked up his bag and, to the utter amazement of his fellow students, walked out of the room and out of the school.

'Raju! Hey, Raju, where are you going?' voices rang out from the classroom. Raju just kept walking.

He thought of his friend sitting in a jail cell by himself. He wondered whether the police had beaten him too. He could feel his stomach clenching at the thought of Tareq being alone and afraid – he knew he would have been. He was ashamed of the tears running down his face, and he dashed them away with his hand.

He walked without thinking, but soon found himself back at the construction site. The workers were just arriving. He entered the fenced area and made his way towards the stairs leading up. The builders didn't notice him at first till they spotted him climbing one of the ladders.

'Oi, what do you think you're doing?' shouted one of them. 'Get down!'

Raju ignored him and kept going. He could hear the man shouting now to the others, but he blocked out the noise. He climbed up, higher and higher, his legs aching with every step. He could see the top of the coconut tree next to the building, and then he passed even that. Finally, he reached the top.

The sound from below receded and the sun shone down on him. He walked to the edge of the roof and looked down. The people appeared small – they reminded him of the ants marching across his exercise book. The height made him dizzy, and he took a deep breath and stepped back. He opened his bag and found the spinning top, and with a flick of his wrist he let it go, watching it spin by his feet.

DON'T SHOOT THE MESSENGER

Aliyah shook out her newly acquired, ultra-compact umbrella. The water clinging to the black fabric sprayed on to the glistening, rain-drenched pavement. She clicked it shut, slid it into its streamlined sheath and popped it into her bag. Half-past ten in the morning and she was already emotionally drained. The next couple of hours were unlikely to bring any respite.

She braced herself and stepped into the café. The combination of the overhead heater in the doorway hitting her with a warm blast of air and the tantalising aroma of coffee emanating from the room beyond momentarily eased the tension from her body. Much as she had expected, it was packed with people seeking sanctuary from the wretched weather outside. The rain was relentless – the sun barely present. London was living up to its reputation of being perpetually cloudy and overcast. If anyone could peer into her soul right now, it would probably prove to be a shade of grey as well.

The room was scattered with an eclectic assortment of chairs and tables – nothing uniform or matching. The pictures adorning the walls were just as random. Black-and-white photographs of films stars jostled for attention next to prints of stark geometrically impossible Eschers and brightly coloured scenic Van Goghs. Carefully careless? Wondered Aliyah, noting that the effect was surprisingly pleasing to the eye – it was a cheerful antidote to the dreariness outside. She looked around at the similarly motley collection of people, some sitting alone reading, some typing away on their laptops, others engrossed in conversation, but most of them nursing various warming cups of coffee or tea.

She spotted Yasmin sitting at a table in a corner, book in hand, earphones plugged in. Her hair was tied into a messy topknot with stray wisps framing her oval face. Aliyah's hand automatically went to her own shoulder-length hair, smoothing out the frizziness created by the moisture outside. At times, the resemblance between her mother and younger sister was uncanny. Both were petite women with high cheekbones and an air of vulnerability. The resemblance, however, ended there. Whereas their mother was soft spoken, gregarious and exuded an easy charm, Yasmin had a feisty personality – to the point of being belligerent. Aliyah, on the other hand, was the only one of her siblings to have inherited their father's appearance, sporting a taller, heavier frame and an air of quiet confidence and capability. 'Delicate' and 'dainty' were not words she had ever heard to describe her. A packhorse amidst a team of thoroughbreds was how she thought of herself.

Aliyah weaved her way through the tables and stood for a few seconds unnoticed by her sister until she pulled the earphones out. 'Boo!'

Yasmin frowned and looked up. Her face instantly lit up at the sight of Aliyah smiling down at her. 'Hey sis! Didn't see you come in,' she said, standing up and giving her a quick embrace and a kiss. Displays of affection didn't come easily to Yasmin.

'Have you been waiting long?' asked Aliyah.

Yasmin looked at her watch. 'Nah, just got here about ten minutes ago. Haven't even looked at the menu. I was pretty lucky to get a table. As you can see.' She gestured to the packed room.

Aliyah took her coat off and sat opposite her. Close up she thought her sister looked a little pale.

'You said Jamal's coming – has he confirmed?' asked Yasmin, pushing a laminated menu across the table.

'Yup, but you know him – he'll be late. I genuinely don't know how he manages at work. Or do you think he reserves that for us?' Aliyah smiled at her sister, her eyes crinkling at the corners and the warmth in them causing Yasmin to return the smile.

'Well, I'm not waiting if he's going to be late. I'm starving. How hungry are you?' said Yasmin, opening the menu.

'Pretty hungry,' she replied. 'All OK with you?'

'Yup.'

Aliyah scanned her sister's face and wondered if she had imagined the slightest hesitation in the answer.

'Is Bro-in-Law looking after Zoe?' Yasmin continued, and Aliyah let the moment pass, nodding.

'He's taking her to the leisure centre for a swim. She's been cooped up in the flat with this weather. Poor baby.'

A hand thumped down on her shoulder, and she looked up to see her brother looming over her. He bent down and kissed both his sisters on the cheek. The scarf around his neck was deftly unravelled and placed on the back of his chair, along with his coat. He sat down next to Aliyah, his long limbs spilling over the edges of the cramped wooden seat.

'Who are you and what have you done with Jamal?' asked Yasmin checking her watch. 'You're on time!' There was a look of mock horror on her face.

'Very funny,' said Jamal. 'Obviously I've been body-snatched. Have you ordered? I'm absolutely famished.' Both sisters shook their heads, amusement written on their faces. The statement was one they were used to hearing. His stomach was like a black hole, seemingly capable of absorbing an endless quantity of food. It was a wonder he stayed as slim as he did.

'How's my gorgeous niece?' asked Jamal, frowning at Aliyah. 'Why didn't you bring her?'

'She's fine. She's with David.'

'At the leisure centre – swimming,' added Yasmin.

'Shame – would have liked to see the munchkin... and David, of course,' he added, almost as an afterthought.

'How about you drop by some time?' said Aliyah. 'She doesn't get to see you guys enough. Anyway, I wanted to have an adult conversation with both of you, minus the kid.'

Yasmin and Jamal looked at her.

'That sounds ominous! What's up, sis?' asked Jamal.

'Let's order some food, then talk,' she said, a sudden seriousness creeping into her voice. She bent her head, studying the menu intently.

Jamal managed to flag down a waitress, and placed an order for two eggs royale, one eggs benedict (minus the ham), two black coffees and a tea. The young woman's sunny demeanour and exuberance contrasted sharply with the nervous apprehension emanating from the three siblings.

It wouldn't have surprised them if the aptly named Bonny had suddenly burst into song.

As soon as the waitress had sashayed away from their table, Yasmin and Jamal turned to look at their sister.

'OK, spill, what's going on?' asked Jamal again.

Aliyah was finding it hard to meet their enquiring gazes, and started unfolding and refolding her napkin.

'You're scaring me,' said Yasmin, her face had lost even more of its colour. 'Are you sick?'

Aliyah shook her head.

'Is it Mum or Dad?' she continued.

'No, no, they're fine – well, physically at least.'

'Oh my God, what's happened?' The nervousness in Yasmin's voice caused it to rise involuntarily.

'The thing is… well, what I'm trying to say is… they're splitting up,' mumbled Aliyah.

'What?' said Yasmin and Jamal in unison, both looking slightly slack-jawed.

'What do you mean, splitting up?' asked Jamal.

'You're joking, right?' said Yasmin, finding her voice.

'No, I'm not joking, Yasmin,' said Aliyah, 'I saw them yesterday and they told me. This time it's serious. Mum's leaving Dad. Ended up spending the whole day with them. Not a fun day.'

There was a moment of silence as the two younger siblings absorbed the news.

It was Jamal who broke the spell. 'I don't know what to say. I'm not even sure how I'm supposed to react,' he said, running his hands through his unruly hair. 'Why…? I mean… Come on, they love each other, right? They've been married for ever!'

'Sorry, it's just a bit surreal,' Yasmin was shaking her head. 'They've been threatening to split up for years – I just thought they did it to wind each other up…' She broke off her sentence as Bonny, her timing as inappropriate as her mood was incongruous, arrived with their tea and coffees. They waited wordlessly till she left their table.

'It's not about whether they love each other or not. They're just not "in love" any more. They've grown apart. It happens.' Aliyah sounded sad, resigned to the demise of her parents' marriage.

Married at the age of nineteen to a man almost thirteen years her senior, Amina Bari had been swept off her feet by her erudite, intense and ambitious husband. It had been an arranged marriage of sorts – the families had introduced them in the hopes of a match – but to catch the attention of the highly sought-after Sohrab Hamid had been exhilarating. Her starry-eyed devotion had charmed him; and both Amina and Sohrab had mistaken infatuation for love. He rapidly tired of her youthful exuberance, and she found him to be devoid of romance, spontaneity and imagination. Her dreams of becoming an artist were cut short by the birth of their first child, and kept on hold by the four that followed. The youngest two had come in the form of twins, and between them the five children had taken up all her time, and her art had receded into the background for everyone except Amina – relegated to a hobby and perceived as whimsy. Sohrab had turned his attention to providing for his larger than expected family and growing his small fund-management business into a multi-million-dollar enterprise. Over the years, Amina, contemplating her own frustrations, often wondered which came first for him – providing for her and the children or realising his business ambitions.

For Aliyah, Jamal, Yasmin, Farhan and Niam, private schools, holidays abroad, an absentee father and doting mother had been part of growing up. Dad was a workaholic and Mum was a dreamer.

'Have you spoken to Farhan or Niam?' asked Yasmin.

'Not yet. I'll call later – I doubt they'll be up anyway,' said Aliyah.

'Oh God! Farhan is *not* going to take this well,' said Yasmin, concern clouding her face. 'He's going to want to come down and talk to Mum and Dad.'

Aliyah was fully aware that her youngest brother would very likely want to hop on the next train from Manchester to London the moment he heard the news. Being a hot-headed twenty-year-old, they would have to broach the topic carefully. The last thing she wanted was any disruption to his studies, or Niam's. Out of the two, Niam was by far the calmer and more level-headed – Aliyah could almost imagine his reaction now. A slow, steady blink, a resigned nod, a stoic shrug and a retreat into silence. She knew his immediate concern would be his mother, although she was just as certain that he would never voice his feelings.

'So Mum is seriously thinking of leaving Dad after all these years?' Jamal had the bemused, incredulous look of someone who had just been informed that the world was in fact flat, and dinosaurs still roamed the earth.

'She's not *thinking* of leaving, Jamal, she *is* leaving,' Aliyah said, sighing. 'I got a call from Mum yesterday and she wanted me to go over. Sounded urgent but she wouldn't tell me anything over the phone, and when I got there they sat me down together and told me. Apart from the shock, it was bloody weird – they're bizarrely formal with each other. Thought I'd be in for a few hours of arguments and recriminations, but it was "thank you" this and "thank you" that, "that's very good of you", "I won't stand in your way"! Dad even ignored his phone while I was there – that must be a first. She says she can move out, as that's only fair. I think she's even found a flat in town.'

'How the hell did we miss this? I mean, if she's found a flat and is moving out, it can't be a sudden thing, can it?' said Jamal.

'I know. Didn't see it coming either,' said Aliyah, although her answer didn't ring true to her ears. Had she really not seen it coming? Or had she just chosen to ignore the signs of her parents' unhappiness? Maybe she and her siblings had been so eager to begin their own lives that in their selfishness they had been blind to the two people they had left behind.

'Obviously it's not sudden,' said Yasmin. 'I mean, if we're going to be honest about it then it's surprising they lasted this long.' She looked at her brother and sister and shrugged. 'Dad's always been busy with work, and Mum's been busy with us and her various "hobbies" since Farhan and Niam went to uni,' she said, forming quotation marks in the air. 'I think they only put up with each other because of us. It's not like they ever did anything together. Ever since we left they seem to have led separate lives.'

Yasmin's words compounded Aliyah's feelings of guilt. The twins' departure for university had left a void in her mother's life, one she tried to fill with hobbies and activities. None seemed to have succeeded in holding her attention for more than a few months.

'How's Dad taking it?' asked Jamal. 'Poor Dad.'

'He's gone very quiet. I think he took Mum for granted – thought she'd always be there. But he's not fighting it. Like I said, they're being – dare I say it – "grown-up" about it.'

'It's not just "poor Dad",' Yasmin said, rounding on her brother. 'He's had a part to play in this as well! I think we all forget that Mum is actually a person – not just "Mum". We probably all take her for granted. Especially Dad. Half the time he treated Mum like a child – and yes, I'm aware that she can be childish at times, but it must have been galling for her to have him do that in front of us. He hardly ever asked her opinion on stuff, and if she ever dared to question him he was all "you don't understand" – so dismissive.'

Jamal leant in, his face flushed. Aliyah could sense what was coming. The old battle lines laid bare.

This time Jamal's voice was tinged with anger as he spoke. 'The guy worked his socks off to look after us. Give him some credit, for God's sake. And Mum never, *ever* took any interest in anything he did. She'd be in some other world the minute he started talking about his business.'

'Nobody asked him to work 24/7! I would have liked to see him occasionally at some school function or the other – or maybe he could have made time to come and see me in hospital when I broke my leg, instead of flying off for some bloody meeting! "It's not exactly life-threatening" – isn't that what he said? And where was he when the twins were born? Oh yes, work. You know I'm right.'

'And you just love being right…' said Jamal, his arms now folded across his chest.

'What's that supposed to mean?' Yasmin said, narrowing her eyes, her voice raised slightly.

'Commitment? Seriously? Rich coming from someone who has an expiry date on all her relationships. Six months – or is it four these days?' Jamal baited Yasmin.

'Better than someone who's still pining over an ex after two years! That's just pathetic. She… doesn't… love… you. Get over it!'

The two faced each other. To Aliyah they looked like they had as kids, trying to outstare one another. In different circumstances she might have found it comical, but by this point she had had enough.

'Seriously, grow up! It's not about either of you. It's about Mum and Dad.' The anger in her voice took the other two by surprise. 'I'm so tired of listening to you two argue the whole time – talk about being self-absorbed! How about thinking of someone else instead of yourselves for a change.'

They turned to look at her, this time with contrition written on their faces.

Jamal was unused to seeing his seemingly unflappable sister so furious. 'My bad. Sorry,' he said.

Yasmin's apology was far more reluctant.

'Look, they both had their faults,' Aliyah continued. 'Maybe they should have done this ages ago – maybe it's for the best – I don't know.' Her anger gave way to a sudden weariness; all she wanted to do was go home and cuddle Zoe and feel David's arms around her. She tried to think of the best way to impart the next piece of information. 'There's more to it than just Mum leaving.' She felt two pairs of brown eyes boring into her. She wished she could do a Houdini and disappear. 'Mum said… she told me that… she's met someone else.'

'What?' the other two chorused, in an instant replay of their previous reaction. Both looked dumbfounded.

'Who? How? Jesus, do I even want to know?' groaned Jamal, his body sagging into the chair.

Yasmin, on the other hand, sat bolt upright, her eyes glittering. 'Go on…'

Aliyah wished her parents had not thrust the burden of disclosure on her shoulders, broad as they might be. 'So, you remember Mum joined an art class earlier this year?' she went on. 'Apparently some of the assignments were to visit art galleries, and she met him on one of her trips. They got talking and…' She found it hard to continue.

'I feel like someone's just put my head in a blender,' said Jamal.

'He's an artist, he's French and he's a bit younger,' Aliyah blurted out.

'An artist? How much younger? Shit, he's not our age, is he?' Yasmin sounded horrified.

'French?' exclaimed Jamal.

'I think she said he's about nine or ten years younger, and he's had a few international exhibitions. Owns an art gallery somewhere in London and one in Paris. I can't believe I'm saying this, but Mum looks happy – I mean, really happy. Her face lights up when she talks about him. And she's started writing and painting. She told Dad about *him* a month ago.'

'Are you OK with all this?' Jamal asked his sisters. 'I'm finding it all a bit hard to digest.'

'Am I happy with the situation? Course not!' Aliyah replied. 'Am I OK with it? I guess so – but it's not like I've had ages to get used to this either, Jamal. I only found out yesterday. Anyway, not much I can do about it. It's been brewing for ages, and we just weren't paying attention. Right now, I just want them to be happy, and they haven't been for a while.

Mum and Dad have to lead their lives – it's not like we have the right to tell them who to be with or who to love. I mean, we're not kids any more. Goes both ways.' Aliyah reached out and held her brother's hand. He looked grateful at the gesture. She wondered whether her words were meant to reassure her siblings or herself.

'Do you know anything else about the guy?' asked Yasmin.

'Not much,' she said, shrugging.

Jamal pulled his hand away from Aliyah and took his phone out of his coat pocket. 'What's his name? I'm going to Google him.'

'No, you are *not* going to Google him! I won't tell you his name. You can ask Mum if you want to know,' Aliyah said.

'How come they didn't want to tell us themselves?' Yasmin asked, sounding calmer than her brother.

Aliyah had been waiting for this question. She didn't have the heart to tell them that their parents, especially Mum, had been reluctant to tell any of the others for fear of their reaction. Instead she said, 'I think they thought it would be easier… better coming from me. At least you'll have had a bit of time to process this before seeing them. Though I think you should go and see them sooner rather than later… I might have told them we'll all go after brunch today.'

'Seriously?' Yasmin looked unimpressed.

'There's no time like the present,' Aliyah said, with a forced laugh that was a mirthless hollow noise.

'You know what,' said Jamal, 'I think I'll go up to Manchester and tell Farhan and Niam face to face.' He looked at his elder sister. 'I think you've had enough drama to deal with.'

66

It was Aliyah's turn to look grateful. 'I think Mum and Dad would appreciate it too. They were thinking of going up themselves once I'd told them, but it might be better if you go in person first. Knowing Niam, he'll give you advice on how to deal with the whole thing.'

For the first time during the conversation, both Jamal and Yasmin smiled.

'I'll head up tomorrow,' he said.

'Do you want me to come?' asked Yasmin, extending an olive branch.

'No, don't worry about it,' he said kindly.

Bonny arrived for the third time, carrying three precariously balanced plates in her hands. Having deposited the correct order in front of each of her three very silent customers, she asked in her cheery voice whether there was anything else they needed and to give her a shout if they did.

'Better eat your food before it gets cold,' said Aliyah. 'Don't know about you, but tepid eggs benedict does not appeal to me.' Her attempt to lighten the atmosphere was partially successful. Jamal smiled and tucked into his eggs with far less gusto than was customary, while Yasmin sipped her tea looking thoughtful.

An unspoken moratorium on the situation had been imposed, and the next twenty minutes were spent eating and chatting about work. Yasmin regaled them with stories of her boss – the editor-in-chief at the fashion magazine she worked at – and her imminent departure; they heard with ever-growing qualms about Jamal's intention to give up his job at the management consultancy and start up his own business; and Aliyah filled them in on the difficulties of managing both a rambunctious three-year-old and a small catering company. Brexit was discussed with much head shaking and a fair few expletives, as was the need for fewer estate agents and more bakeries. A welcome respite, though each was aware that they were all silently processing the news.

'Well, it's been quite the morning!' Jamal said half-jokingly, waving his arms and trying to catch Bonny's attention. 'I think I need more coffee. Any more bombshells you want to drop, sis?'

'Actually…' Yasmin started.

Her siblings turned to look at her.

THE TRUTH ABOUT SAM

The whirring of the fan was surprisingly comforting. If you could get past the noise of the blades continuously slicing through the air, the sound receded into the background, making the dull steady hum strangely reassuring. It was the lack of this humming and the stillness overhead that made Zarin reluctantly open her eyes. Nothing like power cuts and traffic jams to remind her that she was back in Dhaka.

Not having any intention of getting up, she lay on her back listening to the familiar sounds of rickshaws ringing their bells, cars honking intermittently outside her window and of course the unmistakable unmelodious cawing of a crow – sounds she missed when she was lying in the comfort of her own bed in London. Except for the crows. That she most certainly didn't miss.

She squinted at the white expanse above her, which had obviously been newly painted. As far as she could tell, the whole house had been redecorated in honour of her brother, Ali's wedding. After a few moments of gazing at the ceiling, it occurred to her that the fan was slightly off centre. A little to the left and it would have been just right. Being a worshipper of the god of symmetry, this minor flaw bothered her. It was

69

the same type of irritation she felt when Sam messed up her bookshelf, which was carefully alphabetised, or rearranged her colour-coordinated spice rack. She told herself she was the order to Sam's chaos.

Zarin's annoyance was short-lived as the offending object suddenly came back to life, dispelling the brief moment of stillness. The cool air from the fan caressed her face and she closed her eyes. A few more hours till Sam arrived. The thrill of anticipation was intoxicating. They hadn't seen each other for two weeks, and Zarin desperately wanted to go to the airport, but according to her mother there were more than enough people on 'airport duty'. She didn't want to appear overly eager.

A gentle tapping at the door broke into her thoughts.

'Come in,' she said, propping herself on her elbow.

The door opened and a diminutive figure in a bright yellow and blue sari stood hesitantly on the threshold. She reminded Zarin of a colourful little bird. Her hair was slicked back with oil and her head was partly covered.

'Would you like to have some tea now or later with breakfast?' she asked, fidgeting with the door handle.

Zarin smiled. 'Did Ma send you?'

The young woman nodded and smiled back.

'I'll have some tea now and come down for breakfast in a bit. Is everyone downstairs already?'

The woman shook her head. 'I'll go and bring the tea.'

Zarin couldn't remember seeing her at the house on her previous visit, and wanted to ask the maid her name, but the birdlike woman left the room as silently as she had entered, closing the door behind her. She was more ninja than bird.

In an attempt to escape the previous evening's festivities, she had retired early to bed and blamed it on jet lag. It was half true – she had been tired, but the house had been full of people, and her arrival had resulted in much hugging, kissing and more questions than she had the energy to answer.

Zarin got out of bed and stretched. She pulled out a dark-green dressing gown, folded neatly at the very top of her suitcase, and wrapped it tightly around herself, letting the soft fabric engulf her. It looked like it had seen the inside of a washing machine far too frequently. She took a deep breath and smiled to herself. It still smelt of Sam.

The two of them had met at university. It had been the first day, first lecture; they hit it off immediately, having discovered a shared love of all things *Star Trek* and sushi – that and the opinion it could only have been madness or masochism that had driven them into choosing a joint degree in English and History. A year speckled with all-night study sessions, days spent deciphering the meaning of time in *Waiting for Godot* and hours watching every sci-fi movie ever made had contributed to them becoming almost inseparable for the remainder of their degree.

After graduating their lives had taken them on separate paths, with Sam moving to Birmingham to pursue a career in teaching and Zarin staying in London, having secured a much-coveted position in a publishing house. The distance had only cemented their friendship with regular commutes to each other, and after much soul-searching and many a sleepless night she had finally admitted to herself that she was in love with Sam. The guilt of her own admission had been overwhelming. But there was also a part of her that had been relieved to finally allow herself to give into the feelings that had become all-consuming. You didn't choose who to fall in love with.

Zarin walked to the window and pulled back the curtains. The brightness was dazzling, and she shielded her eyes until they were accustomed to the glare.

She stood for a moment, letting the warmth of the sun bathe her face. She could see the nightwatchman yawning and stretching in front of the gates – probably waiting for the day guard to take over from him. What a miserable and lonely job it must be, sitting there all night.

Hashem *bhai*, their long-standing gardener, was already tending to his beloved plants. The bougainvillea framing the portico was in full bloom, and the fuchsia-coloured flowers contrasting starkly with the newly painted white columns looked beautiful. She needed to tell him how lovely the garden was looking. It was good to be home.

By the time Zarin came down to breakfast the rest of the family, except her father, were already at the table. She was surprised by his absence, as he had always insisted that the family congregate at mealtimes. There was a chorus of 'Good morning!' and her niece Anya got up and gave her a hug.

'Did you sleep well, Zarin?' asked her mother, while gesturing to Belal *bhai*, their major-domo, to refill her glass with water.

Zarin nodded and sat down. She wasn't particularly hungry, so she helped herself to a slice of toast and guava jelly.

'Where's Abba?' she enquired.

'Oh, he had breakfast in his study a while ago,' said her mother.

'He'll probably join us in a bit,' interjected her brother Kamal.

72

'It's a shame you went to bed early – you missed all the fun last night!' said Ali.

Her older sister Farah started laughing. 'There was an impromptu dance session – it was a sight to behold!'

'They called this dancing,' said Anya, flailing her arms in the air. There was a ripple of laughter from the others. 'But Daddy was the funniest.'

'Et tu Brute, Anya,' sighed Kamal, stabbing himself with an imaginary dagger.

'I'm not saying a word – considering I have two left feet, I'm with you, Kamal,' said Zarin, looking at her elder brother with affection.

He grinned at her. 'Not everyone is a Michael Jackson, right?'

Zarin had been surprised on her arrival to see how much weight he had gained since her last visit. Her elder brother had always prided himself on his appearance, and had been an avid sportsman in his youth. Life was obviously treating him well, and he looked content, despite his expanding waistline.

'By the way, Wasim's coming over later. He was asking about you,' said Karim. Subtlety was not his forte, and Zarin could see her mother frowning. The room went silent for a moment before everyone started talking simultaneously.

'Well, I'm looking forward to seeing Wasim when he comes over,' she said, trying to hide her irritation with a laugh.

Both Wasim's family and hers had hoped that the two of them would end up together – they still did, it appeared. He had been their neighbour growing up and one of Kamal's closest friends. She had always got on well with him, and regardless of time and distance they had stayed in touch. Her brother kept hinting that Wasim was still single, but she had just ignored Kamal's gentle but obvious attempts at matchmaking.

She had never told them about her feelings for Sam. They wouldn't understand.

Zarin sat back and listened to the lilting voice of her niece as she regaled everyone with the evening's entertainment and the light-hearted banter between her brothers and sister.

She was hiding things from the people who cared for her the most, and her deception weighed heavily on her mind. Her guilt was compounded by the warmth and love she was surrounded by.

Sam felt that their relationship should be out in the open and not treated like a dirty secret, and it was a sore point between them. Zarin wondered if her siblings would look at her in the same way if she told them about Sam. As for her parents, she wouldn't even know how to broach the topic. Farah had followed her heart and married a man her parents had never approved of, and the marriage had been an unequivocal disaster, resulting in a rather messy divorce. It had devastated her parents, and the topic was all but taboo. Her sister always said that living in Dhaka was like living in a fishbowl – everyone was aware of everything you did or said; privacy was a luxury.

After breakfast her mother suggested that they should all move to the living room, and there was a sudden noise of chairs scraping the floor as everyone stood up to leave the table.

According to Ali, breakfast was the only time there were no guests – otherwise there was a regular influx of visitors during the day. People just stayed for lunch or tea, and dinner was becoming quite an elaborate affair, with more and more people dropping by as the big day drew nearer. He was proved right as, within the hour, the room was heaving with friends and relatives.

There was a continuous flow of guests, and by lunchtime the general cacophony comprised of the chatter and laughter emerging from the living room was a sign that the wedding preparations were well under way.

Zarin was engaged in conversation with one of her aunts when she noticed her father walking into the room and then trying to retreat discreetly. His attempt was unsuccessful – Farah spotted him. 'Abba, come and have a look at the saris we bought! Isn't the Kanjivaram beautiful?'

Her father was obviously not as quick as he had hoped – he always said old age was a terrible affliction. He stood in the doorway and acknowledged the greetings from everyone in the room with a wave of his hand. Zarin could tell that this was the very last place he wanted to be – he had the look of a man who was cornered and had no way of escaping the saris and jewellery being thrust his way.

'Yes, yes, they're lovely,' he said, pointing in the general direction of the pile of saris on the coffee table. Zarin watched him with amusement. She knew he had no idea which sari was the Kanjivaram.

She walked over to him and took his arm, then manoeuvred him out of the room towards his study. He visibly heaved a sigh of relief as he entered the sanctuary of his domain, and his look of gratitude was enough to tell her she had done the right thing by rescuing him from the wedding festivities.

She gave him a quick hug before slipping out. The man behind the closed doors was only a shadow of his former self. These days he liked to keep to himself and tried to avoid any social functions if he could. Farah had become concerned about how forgetful he was becoming. Zarin had noticed it too.

Her mother looked up as she entered the living room and beckoned to her. Zarin sat down next to her with a bright smile. It was usually impossible to hide things from her. She desperately wanted to tell her mother about Sam – but to even think of burdening her mother or father with the knowledge of her relationship to appease her own guilt would be selfish. The truth didn't always set you free.

To avoid eye contact she quickly reached for one of the saris and went into overdrive, praising the intricacies of the embroidery and the quality of the workmanship. She was impressed with her own ability to maintain a steady flow of inane chatter.

There was a sudden cheer and she looked up to see Wasim entering the room – his arms laden with boxes of doughnuts. The kids descended on him like piranhas smelling blood – or in this case chocolate icing.

Zarin watched as he smiled and greeted the others in the room. He was by far the tallest man there, and his large frame towered over everyone else, yet he seemed to move effortlessly from one person to another, manoeuvring with ease around the crowded room. When he finally saw her, he walked towards her with his arms outstretched.

'Look who's here!' he said, enveloping her in a hug.

'Good to see you, Wasim,' she said, and tilted her head sideways to study his face. 'When did this happen?' she asked, pointing at the stubble covering his chin.

'About six months, I think – the ladies find it irresistible.'

Zarin laughed. 'Sure they do – whatever you say.'

They sat down on the sofa and he turned to Zarin. She was conscious of Kamal and her mother watching them. She wasn't sure what they were expecting her to do. It was both disconcerting and irritating.

'How are you doing, Zee?' he asked her softly.

'I'm OK, thanks. Just a bit tired. Jet lag.'

'Can't believe it's been a year since I saw you,' he said.

'Really?' Zarin considered the statement, her eyebrows shooting up. 'Has it been a year?'

'Well, it's been too long.' The look in his eyes and the warmth in his voice was unmistakable. 'Zee, if there's anything I can do – whisk you away from all this madness,' he said, pointing at the rest of the room, 'just say the word.'

'I will,' she replied. What she didn't want was to lead him on. 'How's everything with you?'

'All good, thanks. Hospital keeps me busy. Can't complain.'

'So do you do your hospital rounds with an entourage, or do you have a group of minions following you around?' she said, laughing.

'I wish. But no such luck,' he said, with a friendly roll of his eyes. 'When's your friend arriving?'

She looked at her watch. 'I think Mo is picking Sam up – they should already be here; not sure what's keeping them.'

'Dhaka traffic – gotta love it,' said Wasim.

Zarin looked at him. Life would have been so much simpler if she could have loved this man, with the kind eyes and effortless charm. Her family would have been elated. But life had chosen a different, far more obstacle-ridden path for her.

The doorbell rang and she could hear voices in the corridor. There was Mo saying something about the luggage taking a long time to arrive, and then Sam's clear, distinctive voice apologising for the delay. Zarin's heart did a somersault – it was a wonder it hadn't leapt out of her chest.

Sam walked in with Mo.

Wasim turned to Zarin, 'No wonder you've been hiding Sam from me,' he said in a whisper. 'She's gorgeous!'

Zarin drank in the sight of Sam, and realised once again how much she loved this tall, chaotic woman with the lopsided smile and infectious laugh. She got up and walked to the middle of the room where Sam was being embraced by her mother and sister.

'We're so happy you could join us, Samantha,' said her mother. 'I hope the flight wasn't too hectic.'

'No, I actually managed to sleep for most of it,' said Sam, taking in her surroundings, 'but then again, I can pretty much sleep anywhere. It's wonderful finally being here – thank you for having me.'

'Welcome to the madhouse!' laughed Ali.

'Finally,' said Zarin, as she thrust her arms around Sam and hugged her.

BROKEN

The acrid smell of bleach and stale urine hung in the air – a stench that was both unbearable and familiar. Reshmi closed the door behind her and stepped into the bathroom. It was a dingy little space. The small grimy window had iron bars running vertically down, making the room darker and even more enclosed.

She stood in front of the basin and looked in the mirror, rusted at the edges and mottled with age. Her face was almost unrecognisable in the harsh neon light. The carefully applied red lipstick and rouge on her cheeks made the pallor of her skin more visible. Black kohl defined her doe eyes; the two golden flowers adorning her ears shimmered in the flickering artificial light. But nothing could disguise the weariness behind the soft brown eyes, hollow and sunken, making the young woman in the reflection look older than her seventeen years.

The green-and-gold glass bangles encircling her small wrists jangled as she removed them one by one and placed them on the edge of the basin.

A knock on the door startled her and the last glass bangle slipped from her hand, shattering into pieces as it hit the ground. She frowned and cursed under her breath. These particular bangles were special. Zakir had bought them for her.

'Hey, what are you up to? Come on out. Open the door. I didn't pay for you to spend your time in the bathroom.'

'*Baap-re-baap*, you're an impatient one, aren't you?' she laughed, bringing a forced brightness to her voice.

Usually the babus – a term they used for their clients – would come to the compound to visit the girls, but this one liked to have the girls brought to him in one of the local hotels. He paid extra, so her madam was more than happy to send her girls to him. He wasn't the only one – some of the other customers with a bit of money to flaunt liked to show their importance by going to a hotel and not the brothel. At least it got her out of the compound.

Reshmi bent down carefully holding the *anchal* of her sari, making sure it didn't touch the damp mosaic floor, and picked up the broken pieces. She placed them on the side of the basin with their companions.

She loved the little shop nestled within the walled enclosure of the brothel – the small shelves bursting with the vibrant colours of bangles, earrings and hair ornaments. The owner, Loknath, was a toothless old man with a face as dry and lined as old parchment and a ready smile for all the girls. The thought of a visit to his little hole in the wall was akin to a small chink of light in the otherwise relentless monotony of their lives. She was used to the inevitable fight over a pair of earrings or heated argument between the girls vying for the same bangles. Salma Begum, their madam, would usually decide who got the coveted item. Zakir had seen Reshmi eyeing the bangles, and had presented them to her later that day.

The knocking turned into banging, making the door shudder.

'I'm coming!' she called. She stood up straight, taking a deep breath as she reached out and opened the door. Two bloodshot eyes greeted her. The look in his eyes was one she was familiar with – hungry, greedy, lustful.

He grabbed her wrist and pulled her into the bedroom, his hands rough and clammy. She stopped herself from recoiling at his touch. Instead she smiled as she walked into the room. Different room, different man, but the feeling was always the same.

He led her to the edge of the bed and sat down. 'Take it off,' he said, pointing to her sari.

Reshmi tilted her head to one side, allowing her long braid to fall forwards across her breast. She started to unplait her thick hair, her movements slow and deliberate. She wanted to postpone the inevitable for as long as she could.

'Babu, you want me to do all the work, then?' she teased him, forcing a trill of laughter. The sound was as brittle as that of her bangles breaking on the ground.

Slowly she unwrapped the cotton sari from her body, which was now moist with perspiration. She let the garment fall to the floor, a sea of red fabric.

'Keep going,' he said, his voice thick with desire. His eyes never moved away from her. The sight of the checked shirt tight around his wide chest and the brown trousers held up by a belt under his pot belly made her look away. He was old enough to be her grandfather. She could feel the familiar sense of revulsion spreading through her, starting at the pit of her stomach and slowly coursing through her entire body. But she kept smiling. The other girls said it would get better with time. All you had to do was go through the motions – just smile and moan for the clients. One hour and then it was over. But it had never got better – the hour just felt longer each time, especially when she was stuck with a customer like this. For an hour she was his property.

Her hands trembled as she unbuttoned her blouse. Each unfastening of a hook made her heart beat faster. The blouse joined her sari on the floor in a heap. She could hear him breathing heavily as she untied her petticoat. The last vestige of her modesty gone, she looked up.

He was unbuttoning his shirt, his haste making him fumble with the buttons. The trousers came off next. She looked away, but not before she saw the girth of his fat belly. He pushed her on to the bed and climbed on top of her, his weight making it hard for her to breathe. She wondered how many scenes such as this the hotel room had witnessed – whether it had noticed the sadness or pain in the eyes of the girls within its confines. If the girls had kept their eyes open, they would have looked up and seen the same whitewashed ceiling, cracked and peeling with age, the cobwebs hanging in the corners of the room. Maybe they had kept their eyes shut, waiting for the ordeal to end. Reshmi had learnt long ago to close her eyes and think of a song she liked and hum it silently in her head.

The memories of a life before the brothel were fading with time. Sometimes she found it hard to remember how long she had been with Salma Begum. Time had ceased to be of any consequence, each day a continuation of the one before, the days of the week merging into one another. She had a vague recollection of being brought to the brothel by her uncle. Like most of the other girls she had been sold to her madam for a small sum of money – a debt she was still paying off. Life was playing a cruel joke: the girls had to work in the brothel to pay off the debt that had put them there in the first place.

With both her parents dead and buried by the time she was five, she had been left in the care of her *chacha*, her father's younger brother. He had reluctantly taken her in. But for a family with barely enough food to go around she was just another mouth to feed and a burden. By the time she was eight, he had sold her to Salma Begum. At first she had swept floors, cleaned rooms and washed clothes for the others, until she had come of age, when she had started bleeding. Shimul, one of the older girls, had laughed and told her that her body was like a shop – it was now open for business, and she should make the most of her goods. The more money she made the better they would treat her.

Reshmi had learnt very quickly that crying in front of the clients could easily earn you a beating and no food for the next day. 'Be thankful, you ungrateful girl – at least you're not begging on the street or starving,' Madam had said to her all those years ago. A satisfied customer was a repeat customer.

When she had started working she had been given tablets to take regularly – they helped fatten her up. She felt like a cow being fattened before it was taken to the market. The pills also gave her headaches, and made some of the other girls sick, but they still had to take them.

'Remember, no man wants to lie with a girl who's just skin and bones,' Salma Begum would say as she handed them the medicine and waited till she had seen them swallow it before moving off.

There had been a time she had wanted to give up in the same way that the world had given up on her, but a stubbornness inside her had taken hold. Death was an end to her suffering, but surely life had more to offer. She kept telling herself that all she needed was patience.

Zakir had told her he would take her away from this life once he had enough money. It was a dream she held on to every time she was with another man. The first time she had been

83

with Zakir, he had talked to her and tried to make her laugh before the sex. She had felt like a person for a change, not just a body used for satiating the urges of the men who came to her.

She didn't understand why some of the girls chose to stay even after they had paid off their debt. Mona was one of these – she was one the first people who had shown Reshmi a bit of kindness, and had taken her under her wing, making sure the others didn't bully her. Reshmi reminded her of her younger sister whom she hadn't seen since she had been brought to Salma Begum. When Mona had settled her debt she continued working – she was frightened of the world outside the walls and the stigma her past would carry. This was her world: a world she was familiar with. 'Now that I don't have to pay Madam everything I earn I can make some money from the *harami* babus,' she had told Reshmi with a smile.

The man shifted his weight. His face was buried in her neck and she could feel his hot breath on her. A picture depicting a man gazing out across the sea hung on the wall next to the door. She had never seen the ocean, but had heard that it could sound like the rustling of leaves in the gentle breeze, or the roaring of a hundred tigers when the waves rose up and crashed on the rocks. She wanted to feel the sand between her toes and taste the salty seawater on her lips. Maybe one day she would find out for herself if all the stories she had heard were true. Maybe Zakir would take her.

Reshmi closed her eyes and thought of a song she had heard blaring on the radio and began to hum the tune silently, waiting for the hour to finish. She thought of Zakir, who would be smoking his cigarette outside at the end of the hour, waiting to take her to her next customer.

IN CASE I DIE

The phone dropped from my hand. I stared at the limb dangling by my side.

'My arm!' I said out loud – or at least, I think I did. Maybe I said it in my head.

I was standing, perplexed by my arm, and then I was on the floor, kneeling by the bed. My head was resting on top of the mattress. All I could see was the pattern of the pale-blue duvet cover with the orchids embroidered on it. I wasn't sure how I got there or what I was doing. Everything was quiet – as if someone had turned off the sound. The sensation of having the noise muted inside my head was unfamiliar. Calm and Zen-like isn't something I associate with myself. I thought I must be dreaming. I closed my eyes.

I was on the bed, flat on my back – not sure why I was lying down, or how I got here either. Then it felt like the sound had been turned back on at full volume. The noise of the lawnmower in the garden, a television somewhere in the background, people talking. Someone was splashing water on my face. It felt like a lot of water. I tried to move my head, but couldn't, and the water got into my mouth

85

and nose. For a moment, it was hard to breathe. This dream was fast losing its charm.

I looked up and saw my mother and elder daughter. My mother was splashing the water and my daughter was on the phone. They were both crying. I tried to open my mouth, but no sound came out. I tried again, but they couldn't hear me. I could feel a sense of panic rising. Why couldn't they hear me? Why were they crying? Then the thought hit me – was I dead? Surely I must be dead – otherwise why couldn't I speak? Maybe any second my spirit would leave my corporeal body and I would see my lifeless form on the bed. From the corner of my eye, I could see my younger daughter standing quietly at the foot of the bed. She wasn't crying. I waited, but nothing happened – my body and I were still lying on the bed.

Death teaches you a thing or two about life. The first is that there is never a right time to die. It reminded me of the time we took our elder daughter for her booster shots aged five. The moment she came face to face with the needle, she ran out of the room shouting, 'I'm not ready, I'm not ready!' That was me now. I wasn't ready.

I needed to see my kids grow up. How would they manage without me? We like to tell ourselves that we are indispensable to those who we love. But there is also a fear of life going on without us.

What about all the places I wanted to travel to? I always meant to learn a new language, to write my first novel. Why is it that we become so involved in the minutiae of life that we forget to live?

Time must have passed without me realising. When I opened my eyes there was a hive of activity in the room. Had I fallen asleep, or did time just move differently when you were dead? The overhead lights were glaring down. There were three figures clad in green hovering over me and around me. Aliens? I wondered.

Then they spoke. In English.

Not aliens. Paramedics.

'Can you hear me?' said one of them loudly. Maybe I wasn't dead if they were trying to communicate with me.

No need to shout − I can hear you loud and clear, I thought to myself. I tried to say, 'Yes I can hear you,' but the words didn't come out. Just sounds.

'Have you taken anything?'

I frowned. Were they referring to drugs? I was of the 'my body is a temple' school of thought, and had never felt the need to take any mind-altering substances. I'd never even smoked weed in University.

They checked my eyes − probably to see if my pupils were dilated.

'Of course not,' I tried to say. The words came out as garbled sounds again.

There was a definite look that passed between them − I couldn't figure out what it meant.

'Can you please raise your arm?' one of them asked.

Which arm? It suddenly occurred to me that I couldn't see or feel my right arm. I tried to move my head, but it wouldn't cooperate. It refused to budge. Where on earth was my right arm? Why couldn't I see it? The terrifying thought crossed my mind that it must have been amputated − that's why I couldn't see it.

The Zen moment was replaced by a state of confusion and sheer panic. Nothing made sense.

Tears started to fill my eyes, making my vision blurry. They trickled down the left side of my face and into my ear. I hated getting water in my ear when I was swimming, and it wasn't much fun now either. Soon the tears turned into sobbing, and I was mortified by the guttural sound that came from within me. The noise reminded me of a wounded animal.

The three men looked at me, and the panic must have been clear in my face or my eyes. 'It's OK,' the one with the beard said soothingly.

All I could do was close my eyes and pray that this was a nightmare, that it was just a matter of time before I woke up. I had to wake up.

When I opened my eyes, the paramedics were still in the room. Or it looked like two of them were – and I couldn't see my mother or my girls. The door had been closed in the mean time. It wasn't a nightmare – at least, not the sort you wake up from.

I was trapped inside my body. Was 'mental asphyxiation' a term? If it wasn't, it should be. I felt claustrophobic.

The door opened and the third paramedic came back in. It was the bearded one again. He had a wheelchair with him. 'We're going to lift you up and sit you down,' he said. 'Don't worry – we've got you.' He picked me up and another one with blond hair helped place me carefully into the wheelchair. I couldn't see the third one – he was standing behind me.

They had to strap me in, as I didn't seem to be able to support myself. I felt like a rag doll flopping around having my arms and legs rearranged by someone else. I had never felt so helpless.

The ambulance was waiting outside and my family were standing by the door.

'Can we come in the ambulance?' I heard them ask the paramedics. I think they said only one of them could join me, and it was probably best if it was my mother.

Once the three men had got me into the vehicle, they took me out of the wheelchair and lay me down on the stretcher and strapped me in. I was alone for a while. I wondered where my mother was. I thought I could hear the paramedics in the front of the ambulance talking to each other.

It was a relief to think that they were finally going to take me to a hospital. I lay there trying to slow the pounding in my chest. Quite suddenly, my right arm started moving. The rest of my body was still immobile, but the arm raised itself in the air and began flailing around with a life of its own. I had no control. It came down on my face and my hand felt like a dead weight. I couldn't make it move from my mouth and nose. The thought crossed my mind that my right hand was now trying to suffocate me. It was straight out of the *Twilight Zone*. If it hadn't been so terrifying, I might have thought it funny. Somewhere in the back of my mind, I recalled watching a TV serial where the suspect had no control over his arm or hand and was accused of strangling his partner. I had rolled my eyes at the far-fetched medical reasoning behind his acquittal, but here I was trying not to be smothered by my own hand. Unless there was such a thing as a limb being possessed? Talk about 'life imitating art'.

My right hand moved again and bashed into my left hand, which was resting on my stomach. It took every ounce of determination to make the fingers of my left hand move and hold my right hand down. I lay very still, hoping the offending limb wouldn't escape its makeshift imprisonment.

Someone stepped into the ambulance. It was my husband – my mother was not with him. I tried to smile, but I think it might have been more of a grimace. He placed his hand over mine and I prayed that he wouldn't accidentally release my psychotic right hand.

Then the paramedics were back, and I heard them ask him which hospital he thought they should take me to. Odd thing to ask – surely they should know?

'The closest one,' he replied. It sounded more like a question.

The doors closed and I felt the ambulance lurch into motion. I looked at my husband. He spoke to me in a reassuring voice, although I can't remember what he said. I was too busy wondering why he wasn't more distraught. Maybe if he had appeared a little dishevelled or had shed a tear it would have made me feel that he was sharing my panic. Instead he was calm and collected. The rational part of me knew it was his way of keeping me calm, but I was far from feeling rational.

It didn't take long to reach the hospital, and I was swiftly wheeled into A&E. The lights on the ceiling whizzed passed me as they rushed me in. The doctor saw me almost immediately, and he asked the paramedics a few questions and then, like a video on rewind, I was rushed back out of the hospital and back into the ambulance. I felt my panic levels rise again as we drove away.

There was a loud, persistent noise outside that wouldn't stop. As if reading my mind, my husband leant forward and said the sirens were for me. It made me aware of the urgency of our journey. All the while I was clutching on to my right hand.

Finally, after what felt like an interminably long drive, we arrived at hospital number two.

A feeling of déjà vu washed over me as I was rushed through the doors of A&E – only this time the medical staff were waiting for my arrival. There were quite a few of them. Episodes of hospital dramas came to mind. Real-life drama wasn't as glamorous. It was disorientating and frightening.

Things were a blur as they checked my blood pressure, did an ECG, checked my eyes and asked me to raise my arm, then my legs, one after the other. To my relief, there seemed to be a little mobility back in my arms, and my right arm had stopped attacking me and was behaving again. They put a cannula into my arm and started an intravenous drip.

'They've brought you to another hospital,' my husband said softly. 'You've had a stroke. Apparently it didn't present itself as a straightforward case, so the paramedics weren't sure what it was.'

Over time I had been prepared for the likelihood of cancer or a car accident, but a stroke had never even crossed my mind. I was well below fifty. I didn't smoke or drink, wasn't overweight and had never even had high blood pressure. The strange thing was there had been no pain. If I had died, I suppose I could have been grateful that it would have been a painless one.

'Do you know where you are?' asked the consultant, smiling benignly at me.

'Hop-si-tal,' I replied. I tried to correct myself. 'Hop-si-tal.' This time I frowned.

'Do you know what year it is?' he asked.

Yes of course – it was 2016. I tried to articulate this, but my brain wasn't cooperating. 'Two… zero… one… six.' It was as if I had no control over what was coming out of my mouth.

'Where do you live?'

'Mankden.' This time I could see the concern etched on my husband's face.

'Mankden,' I repeated. No, not 'Mankden' – *Camden*, I thought to myself. I live in Camden.

They stopped asking questions.

The 'Acute Stroke Unit' sign greeted me as they wheeled my bed into the ward. There was a buzz of activity while the nurses strapped machines to various parts of my body. They informed us that they needed to keep an eye on my blood pressure, oxygen saturation, heart rate and God only knows what else. My brain was switching off and I could see their lips moving, but realised I wasn't really listening.

Within an hour – at least I think it was an hour, but my perception of time seemed to be a bit skewed – my husband had to leave. The nurses said he could come back the following day, but only during visiting hours – they had a strict policy. I saw him leave the room, and suddenly I felt very alone. I was a little more tearful than

I would have liked, but my emotions were wreaking havoc with my preferred state of staying in control. The Zen-like feeling was a very distant memory.

The room was empty except for one other patient, who was situated across from me. The nurses filled me in during one of the many checks they did on us. I gathered she was on the cusp of turning a hundred years old, and here I was, barely half her age, sharing Room F of the Acute Stroke Unit. Rightly or wrongly, there was a sense of injustice at my situation. I felt rather hard done by.

At some point the lights were dimmed and the curtains were drawn around the bed of my sole companion. I lay back and listened to the dissonant chorus of the machines in the room.

Just as I was on the brink of giving in to unconsciousness, I heard a voice from behind the curtain. 'Oh, Lordy, lordy, sweet baby Jesus!'

I opened my eyes. Who on earth was she talking to? It was unnerving to hear a voice from behind the white fabric that separated us.

Then came the Lord's Prayer in her frail voice: '…And lead us not into temptation, but deliver us from evil…'

What on earth was she seeing behind those curtains? I tried to pull the covers over my face and lie very still, only partially succeeding, thanks to the lack of mobility in my limbs. Why was she reciting prayers aloud? Was Death standing over her, scythe in hand? Or was it just the ramblings of an old woman? Whatever it was, I didn't want to find out.

There was silence for a while, and my body relaxed, suddenly giving into the tidal wave of weariness that crashed over me. I heard my companion resume her monologue behind the curtain, but this time I was too tired to care. Every ounce of energy seemed suddenly to be sapped from my body, and I could barely keep my eyes open. Death may not have claimed me – but at that moment, sleep did.

THE ENLIGHTENMENT OF

RAHIM BAKSH

The water was almost scalding – just the way Mr Rahim
Baksh of 92 Fernbank Road liked it. There was something purifying about the hot jets beating down on his
body. He increased the heat until it was on the verge of
being unbearable, then turned the thermostat the other
way to its lowest setting. The icy water made him gasp.
An invigorating mix of pain and pleasure.

After drying himself, he wrapped the towel around his
waist and wiped the condensation from the mirror before
shaving. He still favoured an old-fashioned shaving brush
and cream. There was something immensely satisfying
about the ritual of dragging a sharp razor across his chin,
hearing the scrape of steel until he achieved the desired
effect – a smooth, close shave. His old barber would have
been proud of him.

For once, he regretted his limited collection of
aftershaves and colognes. He rejected his favourite
and most frequently used, Old Spice, leaving a choice
between the Paco Rabanne and Aramis. After a couple

of minutes of indecision, he opted for the former and sprayed it liberally. The intensity of the fragrance hit the back of his throat, making him cough.

He stood staring at the row of shirts hanging in his wardrobe. They reminded him of soldiers standing to attention. Rahim Baksh believed clothes were for functionality, not fashion. Had it been any other day, he would have reached for the clothes most easily accessible: the trousers that were at the top of the pile and the shirt on the end of the hanging rail. He repeatedly wore the same clothes – something that until today had not bothered him.

He took his time surveying the garments, his hand lingering over a white shirt before selecting a dark-blue-and-white checked one. Then he pulled from the bottom of his pile of trousers a pair of denim jeans. Even as a young man he had never been comfortable in jeans, but his life was about to change, and he felt that this should also be reflected in his appearance. It was to be both an internal and an external makeover. Despite having put on a few pounds, he was relieved to be able to get the jeans on – he had forgotten that the jeans had been a size too big for him in the first place.

There was a pinging noise from his mobile. It was a text message from Karen. His heart beat faster. How strange that just her name should create this excitement.

Have the book I promised to lend you. See you later.
:) x

What caught his attention more than the words or the smiley face was the 'x' at the end. A kiss. She had sent him a kiss.

He closed his eyes and took a deep breath and imagined her heady perfume. He could almost feel her full lips pressed against his own. The kiss, albeit virtual, strengthened his resolve. He had waited long enough – it was time to declare his love for her.

A quick comb of his thick hair and he was ready. These days there were more flecks of grey than he would have liked. A trip to the pharmacy to buy hair dye had ended with him being too embarrassed to hand it over at the counter and leaving empty-handed. His pride had outweighed his vanity.

He had been at the book club for a year when Karen had joined, around eight months ago. One day, during one of the many animated conversations, Richard, a colleague from the IT department, had lamented the lack of bald protagonists. 'Hairists, the bloody lot of them, I tell you,' he had joked. 'Name a hairless hero if you can.'

Karen had jumped in. 'You know, bald men are thought to be very sexy. Look at Sean Connery and Bruce Willis and Ben Kingsley.'

'Patrick Stewart!' Janice giggled.

'They're actors – not characters in a book. See, you can't name one,' Richard replied.

'Who cares?' Karen said, flashing him a smile. 'They're still sexy.'

'Well, in that case, I feel better already,' Richard laughed, rubbing his balding head.

Karen turned to Rahim and whispered, 'Lucky is the man who has his hair beyond the age of forty.' She winked.

Rahim had adopted her words as somewhat of a mantra. He was on the north side of his fifties, but he still had a full head of hair, unlike some of his contemporaries.

He shook himself back to the present. Walking downstairs, he was aware of the clattering of plates and the bubbling of a kettle. The kitchen was to the right, but first he had to manoeuvre himself past the coat rack, which heaved with outer garments. The stand appeared to have a life of its own, multiplying and growing. In most households, people complained of socks disappearing in the washing machine – a domestic Bermuda triangle; once inside the machine, there was no knowing how many would come out. In his home, the coat rack was going in the opposite direction – multiplying, not subtracting.

His wife Shaila was in her dressing gown. Once upon a time it had been a vibrant primrose yellow, but had faded to the colour of jaundice; an unbecoming shade that made her look sallow. The robe was the third member of their twenty-four years of marriage.

She was armed with a frying pan and spatula.

'Tea's nearly ready, and I've made an omelette for you,' she said. The omelette was deposited unceremoniously on to a plate. 'Two toasts or one?'

'Two,' he replied. He took a knife and fork from the cutlery drawer and ripped a sheet of kitchen towel from the roll, folding it neatly into a triangle. He sat at the small kitchen table and began to butter his toast. 'Have you eaten?' he asked.

98

She nodded and sat down on the other side. The smell of fried onions clung to her dressing gown. He wished she would throw the damned garment away.

'*Jaan*, don't forget we have lunch with Shahed and Margret tomorrow,' she said, taking a sip of her tea. In the early days, he had tried to suggest she use 'darling' as a term of endearment instead of '*jaan*' – but she had laughed and dismissed the suggestion, and after a while he had given up.

'I thought I could make some halwa or kheer to take with us, but I can't decide which. What do you think?' she asked.

He wanted to tell her he couldn't care less what she made, considering he wouldn't be joining her the following day – or any other day. He wished she was more like the wives of his friends or colleagues. In all the years they had been married, she had never baked a cake or made any biscuits. It was always halwa or kheer. Instead he shrugged and simply said, 'You decide.'

He had lain awake most of the night trying out different ways of telling Shaila he was leaving her. 'I don't love you any more' felt harsh – but so did 'I'm in love with someone else.' After all, she was the mother of his two children. He thought about the 'It's not you, it's me' excuse, but rejected it. What worried him more was breaking the news to his son, Shabbir, and daughter, Aneela, who were both at university. He had no idea how they would take it. He hoped Karen would be able to advise him on how best to deal with this rather delicate situation.

'I'm a bit worried about Malcolm,' Shaila said, frowning. 'I haven't seen him for a while. Do you think he's OK?'

'How am I supposed to know? I'm sure he's fine. These people don't stick around in one place very long.'

'I wanted to give him some of the rice and korma I made. But even the people at the supermarket haven't seen him.'

Malcolm was a vagrant his wife had befriended, and she was in the habit of supplying him with meals on a regular basis. Rahim was worried that one day he would come back from work to find Malcolm ensconced in the house wearing his dressing gown and bedroom slippers. He was quietly relieved the man had gone elsewhere.

'What time is your book club today?' asked Shaila. 'You know, I was thinking I should join too. We could go together,' she said, not waiting for an answer.

'Twelve,' he said flatly.

'What are you reading now?' she asked. He wished she would stop asking questions. It was more an inquisition than a conversation.

'It's a book by Kazuo Ishiguro – you probably won't have heard of him,' he replied, looking up from his toast and omelette. 'He won the Man Booker Prize in eighty-nine.'

'Oh, didn't they make a film of his book? What was it? *Remains of the Day* – with Anthony Hopkins. I love him. So distinguished, don't you think, *jaan*?'

Rahim frowned. 'Yes, but we're not reading *that* one.'

Shaila nodded and mouthed an 'Oh', her eyes widening as she stared at his legs. 'You're wearing jeans!

Are you feeling all right?' she giggled and touched his forehead.

Her laughter rankled. 'It's better than wearing that thing,' he said, pointing at the dressing gown. 'Have you looked at yourself in the mirror recently?' His jibe found its mark, and her smile vanished. The look of hurt on her face gave him a sense of satisfaction. Shaila's simplicity had been endearing at first, and her love for all things Bangladeshi had amused him; now he found her lack of sophistication and deshi-ness embarrassing. She seemed plain and unremarkable. A middle-aged woman with a penchant for Hindi serials and cooking.

All those years ago, when his mother had placed Shaila's photograph in front of him, he had been taken with her big eyes and wide lips – not beautiful in a conventional way, but a pretty little thing. He had agreed to meet her, and was even more impressed in person. Unlike the other girls paraded in front of him, most of whom were shy and tongue-tied even when asked the most banal of questions, she possessed an air of quiet confidence.

On their first meeting, she had been candid and expressed her desire to live abroad – something Rahim could offer her. Rahim wanted a wife who would adapt to life in England and provide a home for him and his children when the time came. It was to be a mutually beneficial union. With his newly acquired British citizenship and a job at a firm of accountants, he was quite the catch. Shaila's family and his own were equally enthusiastic about the match. His family was relieved he had agreed to marry a Bangladeshi girl – not one of the English students he was infatuated with during his university days.

He soon realised that an arranged marriage did not lend itself to romantic encounters. There were no stolen kisses or passionate embraces prior to their wedding night. She was less adventurous than he had thought, and they had always met under the sharp vigilance of one of her relatives. Their courtship had been brief, and they had married within a couple of months.

He ate the rest of his breakfast in silence as he contemplated spending the rest of the day with the woman who had reignited his passion. He had soon found out that his wife was an unexciting bedmate – even in the early days she had switched off the lights before climbing between the sheets. He wondered whether she lay there during their infrequent lovemaking formulating recipes or creating shopping lists – her wifely duties were fulfilled with the enthusiasm of an automaton. It was no wonder his attention had wandered.

He recalled Rachel from the office. She was the temporary receptionist whose low-cut blouses were such a distraction that Rahim was unable to concentrate when she was around. Then there was Naomi, the nurse at his GP practice. Her trim little body in her white uniform made his body react in a way his wife no longer did. He hadn't had the nerve to say anything to either of them, but he wasn't going to make that mistake again.

'Will you be back for lunch?' she asked, her voice breaking into his thoughts.

'No, don't wait for me. I'll get a bite to eat with the others from the book club,' he replied as he got up to deposit his plate in the sink. Mancini's would be a good place to take Karen for lunch, he thought – unless, of course, she had other preferences. He felt like a teenager embarking on his first romance.

He put on his coat and made sure he had his phone, wallet and keys. The umbrella was rejected for being too cumbersome. England and the unpredictability of its weather was one of the very few complaints he had regarding his adopted homeland.

The air was crisp and bracing. He took a deep breath and smiled. Not long till he was with Karen. He had taken to arming himself with a newspaper to alleviate the boredom of the forty-five-minute bus ride. The journey was one reason why he had wanted to stop going to the book club.

'Hello there! Long time no see. How have you been, sir?' asked Mr Bhatia, the owner of their local newsagent.

'Very well, thanks. How's Mrs Bhatia?' Wasn't she having some surgery? He couldn't remember if it was the knee or hip.

'The doctor said the recovery is a slow process, but she's doing OK. Mind you, she's loving the attention!' Mr Bhatia said, with a smile that revealed the ever-growing gap in his front teeth. Rahim was none the wiser as to the operation. 'I haven't seen the kids for a while either,' he went on.

'They're up in uni. Not back till next month.'

'How time flies,' Mr Bhatia said, shaking his head. 'Say hello to the missus, and thanks for the samosas she made. The kids polished them off by the time I got home!'

'Will pass on the message,' Rahim lied, waving as he left the shop and walked to the bus stop. Shaila appeared to be feeding the entire neighbourhood.

He didn't have to wait long. The bus was almost empty, and he had the luxury of choosing a seat. He went to the back and opened up his paper. After a few minutes of flipping through the pages he admitted defeat and stared out of the window.

Their book group had been brought together by a colleague from work, Simon, who had roped him in, and for a while he found it interesting. When Karen joined she introduced herself and asked if she could sit next to him on the sofa. He had nodded, making room for her. But from then on had ceased to concentrate, his mind wandering as her knee brushed up against his. During their tea break, he had confided in her that he was thinking of leaving the group.

'Not on my account, I hope?' she had joked, touching his arm.

Instead he became one of the most regular members. Karen injected new life into him, her exuberance bringing colour to his drab existence. In her thirties, she was by far the youngest of the group.

He checked the time, and, realising he was early, decided to walk the slightly longer and more scenic route to Simon's house. It would give him the chance to figure out what he was going to say to Karen – though that would have to wait until the club had ended.

He had over the last few months accumulated and stored in his memory every touch, every smile, all their conversations. He wondered if he would be able to sit near her without giving in to the desire to pull her against him and kiss her. He laughed out loud. That would be scandalous.

He stopped at the zebra crossing and looked across the street. The laughter died on his lips. He didn't have to see her face to know it was her. The familiar grey coat, the blond hair tied in a ponytail, the big black bag she always carried. Only she was kissing Richard while his arms encircled her waist. They were too caught up in their passionate embrace to notice him. He felt winded.

He turned around and walked as fast as he could to the bus stop. He perched himself on the edge of the red plastic bench and sat there watching the people get on and off, counting the buses go by... eight... nine... ten. It was only when his back started to ache that he boarded one. It was the twelfth. The journey back felt interminable – longer than usual – with the houses and buildings going past him in slow motion. From the window he sat at, London appeared miserable.

He entered the house and shut the door behind him as quietly as he could. The television was on in the living room. Judging by the soundtrack, Shaila was watching one of her Hindi serials.

'Is that you, *jaan*?' she yelled.

He hadn't been quiet enough.

'Yes – feeling a bit tired, so I'm just going to go and lie down,' he shouted back as he made his way upstairs.

He sat down on the bed, his body sagging with weariness. He touched the fraying fabric of the yellow dressing gown thrown over the pillow. It felt safe and familiar.

There was a ping from his mobile.

Missed you at the book club. Hope you're OK. Will give you the book next time. x

This time the 'x' at the end of Karen's message appeared to mock him. How free and easy she was with her kisses and affection! He closed his eyes again, only this time the image of her body pressed against Richard's played like a video loop. He walked into the bathroom, took his clothes off and turned the thermostat right up. He stood under the shower and waited for the water to hit his body.

MY FATHER'S DAUGHTER

'One more thing – your father will be at Sophia's wedding…
I just wanted you to know.'

There was silence on both sides. Open heart surgery
sans general anaesthetic would have been preferable to an
encounter with her father. At least the cuts would be surgical
and clean, unlike the wounds he inflicted – deep and messy.

'I'll see you tomorrow. Bye, Ma. Love you,' said Maliha,
putting the phone down and sinking back on to the bed.

She closed her eyes and tried to digest this unwelcome
piece of news. The morning had not started the way she
would have liked, and she wished she had just let the phone
ring out. But it had shown the stubborn persistence of a
mosquito buzzing in her ear, persisting for its drop of blood,
or at least to deprive its mark of any further sleep.

Her mother had not been impressed to hear she was still
in bed when she called. What Maliha decided not to divulge
was that she hadn't even heard the alarm go off earlier in the
morning.

Maybe it wouldn't have been such a bad thing if she missed
the flight. Her father was like a hurricane creating chaos
and turmoil in his wake. Every time she had her emotions

under control and told herself she was better off without him he would breeze into her life, oblivious to the pain he was causing.

The older she grew, the less willing she was to put herself through this emotional rollercoaster. Over the past few years, when he had wanted to 'catch up' because he was passing through London for work, she had made herself unavailable. The excuse of long and erratic hours at the magazine was her staple excuse. She had made poor Richard out to be a tyrant and hard taskmaster. The last thing she wanted was to sit and listen to her father regale her with stories of his other family.

It couldn't have been more than five or six times she had seen him since her eighteenth birthday. Back then she had been naïve enough to believe he truly cared about her. That was then – she wasn't naïve any more.

Maliha let out a deep sigh and rolled off her bed. She looked at the clock – just enough time to have a shower. Not enough time for breakfast. The blackened solitary banana sitting in her fruit bowl would have to do.

She put the finishing touches to her packing, rummaging around in her wardrobe to retrieve the bottle-green sari she had glibly told her mother she had already packed. When she found it she threw it unceremoniously into her suitcase before zipping it up and rushing into the bathroom.

She needn't have hurried – the cab arrived late. She checked one more time to make sure the alarm was on and the lights were switched off before closing the front door behind her. The cab driver smiled at her, but Maliha got into the backseat and let him hoist her suitcase into the boot.

She took out her phone and went through her messages. There was one from Richard:

Have a great time and don't think about work! Will miss you.

He had insisted that she should have a proper holiday and not fret about work while she was away. The office would get by without her for a few weeks. That was what worried her – she didn't want them, or rather him, to get too used to her being way. She thought of writing 'Will miss you too', but instead sent him a brief 'Will try!' Even with Richard, her instinct of self-preservation hindered her ability to let him get too close to her. People couldn't hurt you if you didn't let them.

There was a message from Sarah wishing her a safe journey, and one from Sophia, telling her she couldn't wait to see her in Dhaka.

Maliha didn't have the heart to tell Sophia that she simply hadn't wanted to go on this trip. She would rather be settling into her new flat. Her mother had insisted she get a place of her own instead of throwing money away on rent. Buying a place was a commitment she wasn't sure she was ready to burden herself with, but after endless procrastination she had capitulated. Now she was the proud owner of a two-bedroom flat in Kilburn with a new-found respect for first-time home buyers in London and sympathy for those attempting to get on to the property ladder. She was grateful to her mother for helping out with the deposit.

For the time being she had a bed, a sofa and a bookshelf, all of which the previous owner had left behind. The boxes of her stuff piled in each room would have to be dealt with on her return.

She had let herself be bullied into attending the wedding by both Sophia and her mother. Sophia had called her a few months prior to the wedding and made her promise she would be there. Her mother had simply told her that the flat would still be there in a few weeks, while the wedding would not. She couldn't argue with that logic. At least Sophia was one of the few relatives she enjoyed spending time with.

Just the thought of two weeks in the company of the rest of her extended family was a daunting prospect. There would be raised eyebrows, whispering and – worst of all – looks of sympathy thrown her way. Her single status was a topic of discussion amongst some of her relatives, but one she could handle. It was her decision not to see her father or stay in touch with him that had caused such a stir, and it was something she didn't want to discuss with anyone.

Her thoughts were interrupted by the driver saying something to her.

'Sorry?' she said.

'No, no, I'm sorry for being late,' he said. 'The last customer took too much time coming out of the house – but don't worry, I'll get you to the airport in time.' He looked at her in the rear-view mirror and smiled. 'So, are you going on holiday, or is it a business trip?'

She was in no mood for chit-chat. 'Holiday,' she replied.

'Where are you going – India?' He looked at her in the mirror again.

'No, Bangladesh.'

'Oh. I'm from Afghanistan, but I went to Bangladesh about twenty years ago. Very good people there. Your family lives there?'

Maliha rolled her eyes. He really wasn't taking the hint. 'Yes, my mother lives there now.'

'That's nice. You're going to see her?' The driver had a nice gentle voice.

'Yes – we have a family wedding.'

'And your father – he's in Bangladesh too?' he asked.

Maliha hesitated, then said, 'No, he's dead.'

The driver seemed taken aback by her statement. It had probably come out a bit too matter of fact.

He glanced at her in the mirror. 'So sorry, dear.' This time he wasn't smiling.

Mailha had a fleeting moment of guilt about the lie, but it passed just as quickly. It was easier than telling the truth. This was not the first time she had pretended her father was dead. The lie seemed to have had the desired effect, and no further words passed between them until they arrived at Heathrow.

'Here we are,' he said. 'I told you we'd get here with time to spare!' He hauled her luggage out of the boot and deposited it by her feet. 'Have a lovely time.'

Maliha took her suitcase from him and smiled back. She felt bad for being so churlish, and handed him a larger tip than she had initially intended.

She hoped that the seats next to her wouldn't be occupied, but the flight was packed, and every single seat in economy was full. She glanced at her neighbours, and was relieved to see she was next to an elderly lady and a bespectacled young man. If she was lucky they wouldn't be overly friendly or want to chat the entirety of the journey. It could have been worse – she might have been seated next to some middle-aged man who would spend the whole flight consuming copious amounts of free alcohol and would insist on flirting with her – an experience she had had more times than she cared to remember.

The man next to the elderly woman – presumably her son – helped her put some hand luggage away under the seat in front and passed her a bottle of water. Maliha thought he might be the same age as herself, or perhaps a little younger. He smiled at her, and she gave him a perfunctory smile back. The last thing she wanted was to encourage a conversation.

She watched through the corner of her eye as the young man made his mother comfortable, giving her his pillow and taking the blanket out of its plastic cover and gently tucking it around her.

Maliha's mother's decision to move back to Dhaka a year ago to be with her ailing grandmother had left a vacuum in her life. Although they spoke regularly, it wasn't the same. It had just been the two of them since her father had packed his bags and walked out of their lives when she was twelve. Even at university, she had chosen to stay at home rather than move into halls of residence.

She had come home from school one day to find her mother in tears in the kitchen and her father standing in the hallway with his suitcases. Her mother never cried when he went on business trips, and he never took the big suitcases with him – so she could sense that this was more than the usual arguments. This was not going to end with the slamming of a door somewhere.

He had walked over and knelt on the floor in front of her. 'Sweetheart, I have to go away for a while, but I'll see you soon,' he had said, giving her a hug.

She had cried into the coat he was wearing and refused to let go until he disentangled her arms and walked out the door. He hadn't even looked back. Soon the divorce papers had come to the house. He, on the other hand, had not.

She could still remember the smell of his aftershave. Even now, if she smelt it on someone or in the shops, it made her nauseous.

It was remiss of her not to have realised her father was going to be at the wedding. The thought of having to be civil to him in front of everyone else was galling. The rest of the family would be watching like hawks to see how the Mirza family soap opera unfolded.

'Please fasten your seatbelts…' said the voice on the overhead speaker. Maliha took off her shoes before retrieving her book from her handbag, and put her seatbelt on and leant back in her seat.

She opened the book and after a few minutes realised she was still staring at page 85. The words seemed to stare back at her.

Maliha reached in her bag for her phone. Headphones were such a wonderful way of being able to ignore people around you without offending anyone. Once the flight took off she closed her eyes and let the music block out the humming of the engines, the sound of the babies crying and the gentle chatter of the passengers.

Even with her headphones on and a book in her hand, she was acutely aware that the lady next to her was in quite a bit of discomfort.

'Try putting your legs up,' she could hear the young man telling his mother. He looked worried.

She removed her headphones and turned to the lady. 'Are you OK?' she asked.

The lady looked small and frail in the seat. She nodded.

'My mother had knee surgery a while ago,' explained the young man. 'It's still hard for her to sit for too long,'

'Oh, I see,' said Maliha. 'If there's anything I can do, just let me know.'

They both smiled at her.

After a while she got up to use the toilets. It would be prudent to use them while they were still clean, she thought. Luckily there was no queue.

On the way back to her seat, she spotted a small orange bear lying on the floor. Its left eye was missing and looked like it had had its fair share of adventures. There was a little girl sitting in the aisle seat, and Maliha picked the bear up and handed it to her. She beamed at her showing her missing front teeth and Maliha smiled back. There was something familiar about the girl. She had an elfin face with big brown eyes.

Maliha sat back in her seat and took out the in-flight magazine to see what films were on. She could always catch up on some movies if sleep eluded her. The last film she had seen was with Richard. They had spent the weekend holed up in his flat having a movie marathon and ordering in. It wasn't common knowledge in the office that they were seeing each other. Unlike Richard, she thought it would be a bad idea to make their relationship public, especially if things didn't work out. There was also the inevitable office politics to consider.

She looked up and saw the little girl getting up from her seat. The woman next to the girl got up as well. As she turned her head, Maliha got a clear view of her face. Life was obviously having a laugh at her expense. It was her father's current wife. She ducked her head so the wife wouldn't see her, and ended up banging it on the seat in front. For a split second she panicked, thinking her father might be with them – but then it occurred to her that it would have been impossible to miss him if he had been travelling with them.

The elderly lady asked if Maliha was all right.

'Yes, I'm fine thanks,' she said in a low voice.

The girl and the mother must have headed to the toilets. Maliha hid behind her magazine while keeping an eye out for them. She wanted to take a good look at the woman who taken her father away from her. It had been eight years since she had last seen her.

As they returned to their seats, Maliha noted that time had not been kind to the wife, and her face looked careworn, even through the heavy make-up. She was also a few pounds heavier than Maliha remembered. It gave her a perverse sense of satisfaction knowing that the years had been far kinder to her mother. The woman had always seemed pedestrian to Maliha in comparison with her mother's far more artistic temperament. Sarah had once said she found it incomprehensible why anyone would choose someone so commonplace over Maliha's mother. Maliha had nodded in agreement. At the age of fourteen, this show of solidarity had cemented their friendship even further.

Her eighteenth birthday was one she wished she could permanently erase, but it was one that was indelibly imprinted in her memory. The image of the turquoise dress she had been wearing, the smell of her mother's perfume, her father's blazer with the shiny gold buttons – all immortalised in her memories. He had shown up at the party uninvited, and had the nerve to bring his new wife with him. She wasn't sure why her mother hadn't objected. The reason she had given was that there was no point in creating a scene, and he was, after all, her father. She had wanted to shake her mother. The man seemed to have a hold over her that Maliha didn't understand. Was she the only person who could see him for what he was – a self-serving narcissist?

Her friends had been enthralled by the stories of his flamboyant days as a student, and it was galling to watch them giggle at his witty one-liners and fall for his easy charm.

'Thankfully Maliha is a far prettier version of me – don't you think?' he had said. 'I mean, can you imagine the poor girl with my nose!' She could still hear ripples of laughter. 'Don't get me wrong – men should have prominent noses, gives them character,' he said, pointing at his own and winking. 'Not little buttons on their face like that actor – what's his name. Real men have real noses.' More laughter.

She detested it when people told her she looked like her father – though the resemblance was undeniable. They had the same brown eyes and angular face. He was a good-looking man, but that was of no comfort to her.

Even Sarah had been taken by him.

'But you're my best friend – you're supposed to be on my side,' Maliha had recriminated.

'I am!' she had said. 'I promise I won't laugh at his jokes next time or… or even speak to him.' Sarah had been contrite, but the look of guilt on her face had been so comical, both of them had ended up laughing and hugging. There would be no Sarah at the wedding to give her moral support.

What she hadn't told Sarah – or anyone, for that matter – was that her father had taken her aside during the party. 'I have a very special present for you,' he had said, 'but it's a secret, so you can't tell your mother yet, OK?' He gave her a conspiratorial wink.

She wanted to tell him she was eighteen, not eight. 'What is it?' she asked. Part of her had been thrilled that he might actually have brought something special for her, but her excitement was short-lived as he beckoned his new wife – or rather, his ex-secretary – over. He was such a cliché.

He put his arm around his wife, and Maliha felt sick at the sight of the two of them. She looked around quickly to see if her mother had been privy to this show of affection. Thankfully she hadn't.

Her father bent his head and said, 'Sweetheart, in a few months you are going to be a big sister!' He smiled at her, but might as well have punched her in the stomach. The room felt as if it was closing in on her, and for a moment she found it hard to breathe.

His wife had looked at her with a smile that suggested that once again Maliha and her mother had lost. Maliha had turned around and, without a word, run into the bathroom. Her father had looked surprised as she fled, his face tinged with disappointment – another image that was imprinted in her memory.

She had been sent a picture of her 'sister' after the birth, but Maliha had never met her – nor had she ever wanted to get to know her. Her mother had tried to convince her to at least meet her half-sibling, but at the time Maliha had wanted nothing to do with any of them. In the picture he had sent, he was holding the baby close to his chest, smiling down at her. His face was full of love and tenderness. She had ripped it in two and thrown it in the bin.

It was strange to think that the little girl sitting a few rows in front of her was the baby from the picture. She had never considered the girl as her sister – only as a usurper. But here she was, sitting across from her – her own flesh and blood. She even had the same brown eyes and smile. Her sister was almost close enough for her to touch.

Maliha reached over and took a battered leather wallet out of her bag. She opened the flap and unfolded the photograph that was stuck together with some tape. She held the picture of the man and the baby against her chest. Rayna – her name was Rayna. She carefully removed the tape binding the photograph and, for the second time, tore it up, only this time into little pieces. She sat back and closed her eyes.

OVER THE EDGE

Love is both an overrated emotion and an overused word. I love you, I love watching the sunset, love your nails, I love pizza, bye love, sending love – love, love, love. It's as if people are far too lazy to think of an alternative. I have decided to eliminate the word 'love' from my vocabulary. I am fond of you, I enjoy watching the sunset, cool nails, I never say no to pizza, bye [insert name], sending regards. See? Sorted. Love not required.

But today I am going on a date – at the insistence of my sister. Rather than argue with her, which rapidly becomes circular, it is wiser to accept defeat.

My sister's heart is in the right place, but her matchmaking talent requires work. So here I am at Embankment station, on my way to meet Fareed, just to keep her happy. He works in insurance and owns a BMW – a matrimonial prize, I am told. Good for him – but a complete waste of both our time, as this is not going anywhere unless it leads to sex. That I am open to – if he's decent-looking and isn't conversationally challenged, of course. I dismiss the memory of a date she set me up on recently where the bloke suggested I should maybe order the Caesar salad instead of the pasta dish. I promptly added a potato salad *with* my pasta. Needless to say he never called back.

I retrieve my phone from my jacket pocket and check the time. It should take me ten minutes to walk to the restaurant, so no rush. I slip the phone into my bag.

The air is crisp, unlike the stale smell of the underground. There is a hint of autumn around me, the trees turning from green to russet. I begin to make my way down the steps and trip, landing on my knees, palms out to stop my fall. Luckily there are only four steps. I curse out loud at my clumsiness.

'Is that supposed to be a yoga pose? Downward dog?' a voice says, with unhidden amusement.

It's Benji. Benjamin bloody Godwin. He's leaning on the wall at the top of the stairs, his black hair flapping in the gentle breeze. 'Need a hand?' His arms, however, are crossed over his chest.

I ignore him as I reach out and hold on to the iron railing to hoist myself up, cursing again as I brush the dust from the pavement off my clothes. There is a gaping hole in my tights exposing my knee, a smear of blood on the surface of the skin. I should have stuck to my 40 denier tights instead of these flimsy barely-there ones. No major damage done, other than to my pride.

'Hurt yourself, did you?' he continues. The faux concern makes me want to slap the smirk off his angular face.

My bag is on the ground next to me. Fortunately the contents are still tucked away inside. It would be mortifying to have my life spread out on the stone steps for the world to see – and judge. Phone, house keys on a bejewelled elephant keyring, lipstick, solitary sanitary pad for emergencies, scrunched-up tissues, a half-eaten KitKat. I wonder what those women who I pass on my way to work store in their oversized shiny designer bags. Definitely not scrunched-up tissues. A woman in a long white quilted coat asks me if I'm OK and I nod, smiling at her. The other people are staring into their phones, oblivious to their surroundings, for which I am thankful.

Benji is beside me, his hands shoved in his pockets. 'You can't go around looking like that. You're a flipping mess. What's your date going to say?'

I know he is baiting me, but I can't help myself. 'Shut. Up. I am so tired of you talking – all the time.' My voice is raised, fingers mimicking his yapping mouth.

A couple who are on their way into the station stop mid-conversation, laughter suspended, and exchange glances, hurrying past me.

'People are going to think you've lost it. But that would be true. Right, darling?'

I take my phone out of my bag and hold it up to my ear, pretending to talk into it. 'I can't believe I was ever in love with you. I must have been mad.'

I wasn't always anti-love. But life teaches you lessons, and some of them have enduring consequences.

* * *

Benjamin Godwin was the new guy at work. The one who had been hired to shake up the organisation, bring it up to speed – take it into the twenty-first century.

'He's a bit of all right,' Jane said to me in a whisper. 'He can take me into any century he wants,' she added, fanning herself.

I was never going to admit that I agreed with her. Not that he noticed either of us. We tapped away on our computers, invisible to those higher up in the food chain. That is, until I got caught in that cursed downpour.

It was as if the skies were weeping. I tried booking an Uber and failed, so I stood by the glass doors of the reception area waiting for the rain to recede. Benjamin sauntered past and stopped. I think I held my breath when he came back and raised his eyebrow. 'You're James's assistant, right?'

I nodded like one of those bobble-head toys.

He introduced himself and I took his extended hand. 'Benjamin Godwin. Though my friends call me Benji – you know, Ben G,' he explained. He had a warm, strong grip.

'I'm Rubina. My friends call me Ruby,' I said.

'So where're you headed? Let me give you a lift, Ruby.' He looked into my eyes and I went weak at the knees. He didn't know where I lived, but he was offering to take me home.

At first I declined, saying it would be inconvenient for him, and he didn't have to put himself out on my behalf.

'Look, this,' he said, pointing to the deluge outside, 'isn't going to end any time soon, so let me drop you off. Don't worry, I'm not a serial killer.' He laughed, baring his small teeth. His smile was not his best feature. There are some men who should keep their mouths shut, either because of the voice that comes out or the words they choose. In Benji's case the reason was his teeth.

'Well, you'd hardly announce it if you were one, unless it was a double bluff,' I joked, and promptly accepted his offer. His car was in the underground car park. He opened the door for me. Inside it smelt of leather and aftershave – his aftershave – and I breathed it in.

'So where are you from?' he asked, glancing at me sideways. 'Let me guess. India?'

'No. I'm half Bangladeshi. Dad is English and Mum is originally from Bangladesh. She was born here, but my grandparents moved here in the sixties.'

'That's why you're so beautiful.' He smiled at me, but with his mouth closed. I shouldn't have been flattered, because I am not beautiful – a bit on the chubby side, eyes that were called bug eyes in school, wide mouth. My long, thick hair is my crowning glory, and that's about it. But I was foolish, and I was flattered.

He was surprisingly chatty, and we hit it off immediately.

He was into jazz, loved to travel and confessed he was a secret *Strictly Come Dancing* fan. We ended up fixing a date to go to Ronnie Scott's together. He took my phone and entered his number. I could hardly believe my luck.

And that was where the madness began. We started seeing each other regularly. Dinners after work, movies at the weekend. He wasn't pushy about having sex – though it did make me wonder if he wasn't attracted to me. You can't help but wonder. I would have liked it if he found it hard to keep his hands off me. But I put it down to him being a gentleman.

When it happened I tried not to think of all the women before me. I wished I had taken up the three months' free gym membership offered by the office. You can't hold your stomach in during sex. I tried more than once and failed.

I once made a joke about my love handles, and he smacked my arse and said, 'I like a woman with some meat on her bones. It's sexy. See, you'll still have your youthful looks when all those scrawny model types are shrivelled and wrinkled.'

'Flatterer,' I said, smacking his arse in response.

At work we kept it professional. He would come by my desk or drop me a line to ask for a particular document or give me some work – which technically I wasn't supposed to do, as I was James's assistant. Jane would pretend to swoon behind his back. I felt a twinge of pleasure – or maybe it was pride – at the thought that he was with me: he was mine. Obviously I couldn't tell her.

I began to plan what life with Benji would be like. A flat near Borough Market, jazz nights, holidays in Majorca – it would be perfect. I wondered whether I would change my name. Rubina Godwin. It didn't trip off the tongue, but I still liked the sound of it. I tried different signatures. Jane almost caught me at it, but I managed to scrunch up the piece of paper and throw it in the bin just in time.

I had to give up my lunch breaks to do the extra work. But how could I say no when he looked at me with those soulful eyes? Every now and then Benji would ask me about James and the work I did for him, telling me how lucky James was to have me as his assistant.

Six months and twenty days later he dumped me. Just like that. Stopped taking my calls, blanked me, looked through me at work. James got fired and Benji got his job. I was assigned to David as his assistant. I saw the petite blonde from HR cosying up to Benji, and it made me feel physically ill.

The humiliation was crushing, like a rock that had been placed on my chest and wouldn't allow me to breath. I took sick days so I didn't have to see him. The saving grace was that no one else seemed to be aware of our relationship. I thought I had finally found that one person who would do what all the others before him hadn't done: love me for who I was. That word again – love. The word made me want to throw up. His rejection created a hole in my chest that encompassed my entire being and became an abyss.

* * *

I walk as quickly as I can, hoping to get rid of Benji. But he just keeps pace with me. 'God, one of these days, I swear I'm going to…'

'Going to what?' he goads. 'Kill me?' He purses his lips, his eyes narrowing as if in deep concentration. Then suddenly he swats the phone out of my hand. 'Didn't see that coming, did you?' he crows.

The blood drains from my face. I did not see that coming. I am right in thinking I had felt a hand on the small of my back when I fell – he pushed me. I hadn't just tripped.

'Ever see the film *Ghost*?' he asks.

Yes I have, though he's no Patrick Swayze. He doesn't wait for me to answer.

'I've been working hard. I'm getting there. Ruby, Ruby, Ruby, I'll be by your side, day and night. It's what you wanted, right? Till the day you die, darling.' He smiles at me, and this time it is not his teeth that make me recoil, it's the malice in his eyes.

How is it even possible? I bend my head to put my phone back in my bag and to hide my fear.

He had been smoking in the stairwell. There was a window someone had managed to open on the fifth floor and the smokers went there when it was too cold to stand outdoors. The smoke alarm didn't work, and there was no CCTV.

I followed him, just wanting to find out whether I had done something wrong, if he had cared for me at all or whether I was just a means to an end.

'Ruby, darling,' he had said, 'it was fun while it lasted, but you couldn't have seriously thought that you and me…?' he pointed at me then himself, eyebrows raised.

I hadn't planned it, but his mocking tone and the laugh that accompanied it pushed me over the edge, and I pushed him over the ledge. I had to stop myself from screaming, but after a moment of sheer panic a sense of calm came over me. I ran up the stairs to the sixth floor. No one saw me – or at least, no one noticed me. At times there are benefits to being insignificant: it makes you invisible. I made myself a coffee and walked back to my desk. I had to control the tremor in my voice when Jane asked if I had plans for the weekend. I told her I might visit my sister.

When Benji's death was announced at work, it was the only topic of conversation for the next fortnight.

For weeks I expected the police to show up at my door. I had images of being led away in handcuffs. Face plastered in the papers. Then his fall from the open window was ruled an accident. The window was permanently locked.

When the case was closed, it was as if my lungs had filled with air and I could finally breathe – could move on with my life. But three months after 'the incident' I was at home lying in bed, just at that sweet spot between sleep and wakefulness, when I thought I saw something move in my room. It wasn't something – it was Benji. Standing by the foot of my bed. Then he was gone. I switched the lamp on, chasing away the darkness. I told myself I must have imagined it. It was impossible to sleep after that, so I made myself a cup of hot chocolate and watched some late-night telly.

But two days later he showed up again. When I opened my eyes, his face was peering down at me. I screamed. But this time he didn't disappear, he just grinned. I screamed a fair few times after that, because he would just show up unexpectedly. I have had to train myself not to react when he does, especially as no one else can see him except me.

Five months later, he is still hounding me, showing up everywhere I go. He is even more arrogant dead than he was alive.

I turn to tell him to leave me alone, but find that I *am* alone.

'Till the day you die...' His words echo in my mind, leaving a chill in my heart.

THE LIVES OF OTHERS

Manik looked across the street at the small queue of people forming outside the American Embassy. They were gathered together under the gaze of the row of palm trees that stood erect and tall within the high walls, like sentries guarding the red-bricked fortress.

He squinted up at the guardians of the enclosure and wondered if anyone ever bothered to eat the clusters of green coconuts hanging precariously from the top of the tree, or if they just fell to the ground and were swept away to be thrown into the garbage. That would be a shame. It had been a while since he had tasted fresh coconut water or bitten into the sweet white flesh hiding beneath the green shell.

It was still early in the day, and there were only a handful of people milling around the entrance, but he wanted to get to them before anyone else encroached on his turf. There was one woman in particular who showed up almost every day carrying a baby, but she seemed to be late today. It was strange how a crying baby made the foreigners give money without hesitation; they were always opening their wallets and bags and handing her five, ten and twenty-taka notes. He had seen one of them give the woman a tin of baby milk powder. He was sceptical as to whether she had actually fed it to her baby; more likely she had just sold it. If he was lucky the woman and her baby had moved on.

Every now and then, the foreigners going in and out of the embassy would give him some money as well, although not as often as the woman with the baby. He thought he made them uncomfortable, though one time a lady had given him a hundred-taka note. She had short hair like a man, and had smiled at him with big white teeth. He had never seen teeth that white and even.

As he looked on, a car pulled up and a young woman jumped out. She wore a blue sari and her shiny black hair cascaded down her back, well below her small waist. She waved at the person inside the car, tossed her head back and laughed. People didn't laugh much outside the embassy. They always looked worried – almost scared at the thought of entering the building. He wondered what lay beyond the red walls as he watched her walking towards the group of people.

He gulped down his cup of tea. The hot liquid scalded his tongue.

'Slow down, Manik Miah, what's the rush?'

'Too late, Asad *bhai*,' smiled Manik. He slammed his cup down on the rickety wooden bench and let out a contented sigh. Strange how the hot cup of tea managed to quench his thirst, even though the summer sun was already bearing down on them with all its might. It hadn't rained for over a week and the ground was parched. The dust had settled on the leaves, and the trees looked dirty.

What he could do with now was a cigarette − especially one of those foreign brands, not his usual deshi ones that always left his throat raw but nevertheless felt damn good with every puff. Right now he was out of money. He could ask Asad *bhai*, but the man had done enough for him. It just didn't feel right.

When Manik had first arrived in Dhaka he had been overwhelmed by all the noise and all the people. The city was heaving, and at times he found himself barely able to move through the crowds. It was an ocean of nameless faces. But one thing he had discovered was that there weren't many people like Asad *bhai*. If there were, he hadn't met them. The tea-shop owner had always been good to him from the time he had landed up in the Baridhara area. Since then he had lost count of the number of times Asad *bhai* had passed him a cup of tea or handed him *paan* or a toast biscuit and refused to take any money in return. He said Manik reminded him of his son. He had lost him a decade ago. Typhoid had seen to that. The man had a big heart, and the last thing Manik wanted to do was to take advantage of his friend.

It felt like a lifetime since he had left home with nothing but his dreams, four hundred taka in his pocket and a determination to make something of himself. He didn't want to end up like his father, working till he dropped dead from hunger and fatigue, or his mother, who had spent the last few months of her life beating her chest and shedding tears for his father and the children that had not survived their first year. Manik had watched her weep till there were no more tears left inside her frail body and she had followed his father to an early grave.

'I better get to work,' said Manik as he handed Asad *bhai* his empty cup.

He bent down to pick up his crutches and winced. The pain in his leg was back and had been troubling him the last few days. Night-time was even worse. He had been waking up in agony, a searing pain shooting through his leg, but when he looked down all he could see was his grotesquely deformed stump.

Things had not gone as Manik had planned. Life had got in the way of his dreams –life and a large yellow truck. He sucked in his breath and slowly let it out.

Asad *bhai* looked at him with a frown on his pockmarked face. 'Are you sure you don't want to sit for a few more minutes?' he asked.

Manik raised his hand and shook his head. 'No, no, I'm fine.'

'Hmm,' said Asad *bhai*, not convinced. He swatted a fly away from the bananas hanging from a hook on the side of his stall.

'So what do you think about this new lot?' Asad *bhai* said, pointing to the people across the road. 'Who do you think is going shell out, and who's going to tell you to bugger off?'

Manik grinned at the tea-shop owner. 'Sometimes you're too much, Asad *bhai*! If I could answer that I'd be a rich man.'

'I'm just asking. You've been doing this for a while, so I thought you might have some sort of gut feeling.'

'No, not really – it's just a question of luck.' Manik paused to stare at the line of people. 'OK,' he said after a moment, 'let's see what kind of fish we have in our net today.'

Towards the end of the queue was a middle-aged man wearing a dark brown suit. He had a shiny black briefcase in one hand and a mobile phone in the other. He checked his watch, looked around at his companions and then walked purposefully towards the security guard and said something to him. The security guard didn't look very impressed, and gestured with his hand to go back to the queue. The man looked as if he was about to say something, but stopped and turned on his heels and strutted back to join the line. He put his mobile in his pocket, where he exchanged it for a handkerchief and mopped his forehead and balding head.

'I think the *shaheb* in the brown suit is probably some small-time government official who thinks he's a big shot,' said Manik.

'How can you tell?' asked Asad *bhai*.

'Trust me – I've seen many of them in my time. Who else would wear a suit in this kind of heat or try and push to the front of the queue when everybody else is waiting to get in as well? I wonder what he's doing here.'

'Maybe he's here for some work – or maybe he wants to go and see Obama *shaheb*!' suggested Asad *bhai*.

Both men laughed.

'I thought people like him have other people to do things for them. I'm surprised he didn't bring his peon to carry his briefcase or wipe his face for him!' grinned Manik. 'That kind of person has his wallet under lock and key, and I don't think there's money to be had from there. That, my friend, is a slippery fish.'

'OK, how about the two men standing over there – the one in the white shirt and the short fellow in the grey T-shirt and jeans?' Asad *bhai* pointed in the general direction of the group. His large hands reminded Manik of the bunch of bananas hanging in the shop.

Before he had a chance to answer the question, a man strolled towards the tea stall and addressed Asad *bhai*.

'One packet of Star cigarettes and a tea,' he said in an unusually soft voice. Somehow the voice and the visage were at odds with each other.

Manik stared at him in admiration. He had a magnificent moustache. The ends extended downwards at the corners of his mouth, right down to his chin. Even his grey hair was perfect. Thick and wavy, and slicked back with oil. Manik had only seen moustaches like that on actors – in the days when he had the money to go to the cinema. He figured that the man must have been a driver for one of the people across the street. The drivers would often drop off their passengers and come around to park on the stretch of road next to Asad *bhai*'s tea stall. Some of them even gave Manik a taka or two.

He laid his crutches back on the ground and waited for the newcomer to pay. He ran his fingers through his thick, curly hair; it was coarse to the touch and longer than he liked. No wonder he felt so hot all the time. When he was a young boy his mother used to massage oil into his hair and tell him it made his head so hot you could cook an egg on it. It was one of the few memories he had of her laughing.

When he had arrived in Dhaka five or six years ago, he had allowed himself the luxury of going to the barber every few months with the money he had saved. He had hardly believed his luck when he had got the job working at the petrol station in Kawran Bazaar only weeks after he had arrived. At the time, he had believed that somebody was watching over him. It was long hours and the pay wasn't great, but it gave him enough to live off and save a little bit at the end of the month.

Looking at the man, Manik could feel his admiration turning into pangs of envy and resentment. That could have been him – it should have been him – but his hopes of becoming a driver had faded away the minute his rickshaw had come face to face with the three-ton yellow truck.

Asad *bhai* gave the man his change and turned back to Manik. 'So what do you think?'

'Think about what? Oh yes,' he said looking across the street. He tried to dispel the image of steel tearing into flesh and bone.

Manik shifted his position on the seat to get a better look. The man in the grey T-shirt and jeans had a large envelope under his arm and was staring up at the walls of the embassy. Manik wondered if he was thinking about the fate of the coconuts as well. The young man in the white shirt was looking through some papers he had taken out of a plastic bag.

He chewed on his bottom lip. 'That's a difficult one. Most of the younger ones seem to be students, and half the time they give me money because they feel bad for me and the other half of the time they just ignore me. In fact, once a boy didn't believe me and wanted to see if I really had a leg missing or if I was just holding it up under my *lungi*!' He laughed, but this time his laughter sounded hollow and forced even to himself.

Asad *bhai*'s voice rose in anger. 'What a bastard!'

The man with the moustache looked startled, and turned around to see who Asad *bhai* was swearing at.

'You know, Asad *bhai*,' said Manik, 'when I first started coming around here, around the embassy, people would sometimes give me money and ask me to pray for them. Maybe they thought I had a direct line to God because I beg for a living, or maybe they thought that God feels sorry for me because he took my leg from me. Who knows? One time, when I began working in this part of town, I asked one of the young men standing outside the embassy what he wanted me to pray for and he asked me to pray that he got his "visa". I didn't know what he meant. He explained to me that all those people who stand outside have to get permission to go to America and the people working in the embassy decide their fate.'

'Yes, I know,' said Asad *bhai*, shelling a few peanuts and putting them in his mouth. He took a few more and handed them to Manik. He tilted his head to the side and folded his arms across his chest.

'I've spoken to some of the people who come to the embassy. Now and again the younger ones from the queue come over to buy a bottle of water or something from me while they're waiting, and when I'm not busy I like to have a chat with them. Some of them tell me that they want to go and visit America; others want to go and study over there. I don't know why they're so desperate to go to a foreign country – what's so great over there? Why can't they just study here? I wouldn't want to go so far away. I'm happy in my own country!' said Asad *bhai*, shaking his head.

Manik knew what it was like to be young and hopeful. After his parents had died there was nothing left to tie him to the village he had grown up in, and it hadn't taken him long to decide that Dhaka was where he wanted to be. He could still remember the incessant crowing of a cockerel the day he had finally left his home. The rain had washed away the early morning dust, and the air around him had been heavy with the smell of wet soil. He had walked a couple of miles from his village to the bus station and found a seat on the overcrowded bus heading to the capital, wedged between a man smelling of onions and a man who kept falling asleep on his shoulder. None of that had bothered him, and he had revelled in the excitement of embarking on the journey of his life, ready to make a new start – a new life in a new place. To him, Dhaka had seemed as far away and exciting as America was to these young men and women. He wasn't sure Asad *bhai* would understand.

The man in the white shirt dropped one of his papers and an elderly gentleman behind him picked it up and gave it back to him. He wondered whether the man in the white shirt or the man in the grey T-shirt would get the chance to fulfil whatever their dreams might be, or whether they would be crushed within the red walls of the embassy.

'I hope the boys will be feeling generous today,' said Manik, 'but usually the women are a little more willing to give me something.' He looked at the girl in the blue sari. She was talking on her mobile phone. He could see the bangles on her wrists glinting in the sunlight.

'Ah, that's because of your pretty face, Manik Miah,' snorted Asad *bhai*.

Manik smiled back at him. In the days before life had screwed him over, before his stump, he had had his fair share of attention. The girls in the village would look shyly through their lashes at him and giggle when no one else was around. It was a great feeling. He had been born with fairer skin than both his mother and father, and was taller than the boys his age in his village. But now he was only half a man – no woman would even look at him, unless it was with pity in her eyes.

The man with the moustache looked at Manik. He had obviously been listening to their conversation. '*Bhai*, if you can spare a prayer, you should pray for my *shaheb* and madam,' he said looking almost tearful.

'You see that lady in the grey sari and the man standing next to her?' he said, pointing to a couple standing across the road. 'They are such good people, and don't deserve to suffer like this. They're trying to go to America to bring back the body of their son. Can you imagine how terrible it must be for them, waiting over there, praying that the embassy people let them go to their country to bring him home?'

'*Ahha*, that's so sad. What happened?' asked Asad *bhai*.

'They got a phone call yesterday morning from America. *Choto shaheb* was driving and there was an accident. He didn't even make it to the hospital.' A fat teardrop rolled down his face and disappeared into his moustache. 'I saw *choto shaheb* grow up in front of my eyes…'

Manik shook his head in sympathy. He looked at the old couple standing in the sun waiting for the doors to open. They looked a little lost and bewildered. The man was leaning on a walking stick. Even if they didn't give him any money he would pray for the couple. He thought of their son, who had breathed his last in a foreign country without his family around him.

When Manik had regained consciousness in the hospital after his accident, he had been alone. He couldn't remember how he had even got to the hospital. He woke up in excruciating pain to the sound of other people screaming out in agony. The nurse told him he had been lucky the accident had occurred near the hospital, and two passers-by had brought him in. He didn't feel lucky.

Initially the pain had been so acute he hadn't even realised there was nothing left beyond his knee. The impact of the rickshaw and the truck had crushed his lower leg, and the doctors had not been able to save his limb. At first he wished that the truck had crushed his body, and not just his leg. He had lost track of the number of times he had cursed his so-called saviours for bringing him to the hospital. Why couldn't they have just left him on the road to die? His body had betrayed him and he had survived and recovered. The next few years had been spent watching everything he had worked for disappear. He had lost his job at the petrol station and had been unable to pay the rent for his room. The streets of Dhaka had become his home and the sky his roof.

He was brought back from his reverie by a car honking at an old man trying to cross the road. A few more cars had stopped outside the embassy, and some of the passengers stepped out to join the already existing group of people. By this stage, the line had grown to almost a dozen people. The security guard yawned, his arms outstretched, and got up from his seat. They all looked at him expectantly. Even the guard had power over these people.

Manik had seen hundreds, possibly even thousands of people standing in the same queue, day in and day out, over the last few years. Every day there would be a new group of people standing in the heat or the rain, waiting, hoping to get their visa to go to a country he would never know or see. Whenever he looked at them he didn't feel like the only one who was begging.

'I have to go,' he said. 'Otherwise they'll head inside and I'll miss my morning income!' He straightened his *lungi* as he got up. He wondered whether the girl in the blue sari would give him any money or whether she would look at him with pity. Maybe she would just look away with disgust.

Manik looked at his friend. 'Asad *bhai*, do you think anyone eats those green coconuts inside the embassy?'

Asad *bhai* shrugged.

LET ME GO

The light is fading in the room and I stop reading my book to gaze outside the window. Another day, another sunset. This time the fusion of oranges, pinks and blues is worthy of an artist's canvas. If only I could paint – I would immortalise this moment. Sadly I am no artist, so my memory will have to suffice. A few moments and then dusk starts to fall on the world outside.

Despite the overhead lights the room feels dim – rather miserable, if you ask me. I reach over and switch on the light by the bed. It flickers momentarily then comes on. I look at the face resting on the pillow. The harsh glow of the artificial lights give him a greyish pallor. The tubes emerging from his mouth and nostrils obscure part of his face. He is barely recognisable with the purplish bruise around one eye and gash on his forehead.

His eyes are still closed. They have been closed for over a week now. After the car accident, the doctors decided to put him in a medically induced coma. They told me that his head injury was severe and there was swelling on the brain. According to them, this was the best way to let his body try and heal, although from what I can tell they think the chances of him regaining consciousness are slim.

It was disconcerting at first, but over the last week or so I have become accustomed to the noises the various machines surrounding my husband constantly make. The rhythmic beeping of his heart monitor, the whirring of the ventilator – it's all background noise.

I stand up and the book on my lap falls to the floor with a slight thud and slides under the bed. I can pick it up later. One of the nurses said that talking to him or reading aloud might help, so I bring a book with me to the hospital to help pass the time.

My lower back and shoulders are aching from all the sitting, but even with a bit of stretching and walking around the room the pain remains obstinate. Give it time and your body turns on you, and the things you used to take for granted become herculean tasks. Everything starts clicking and creaking like an unoiled machine. Right now I feel more like a hundred and five than fifty-five.

The hands on the clock above the door of the room are moving particularly slowly today. I think the clock is mocking me. Even the seconds seem to be moving in slow motion. 'Ha ha ha just six o'clock,' it says.

Two more hours and I can go back home.

Even after thirty-five years I can hear my mother's voice telling me I've made my bed and must, therefore, lie in it. I was foolish, immature and oh so stupid to have been seduced by a few sweet words and a roguish smile – I have no one but myself to blame.

A fumbled encounter in the back seat of a car with a man who swept me off my feet gave me one of the best things in my life – my son. Back then, however, people didn't look kindly on unwed mothers, and I thought I was the luckiest girl alive when he said we should get married and be a family.

'No child should come into this world without having both parents,' he used to say.

My second son came soon after the first, and I felt complete. I had everything I wanted.

Unfortunately, time taught me that the man I had given my heart and soul to didn't really love me. I just kept deluding myself into thinking that he did.

Well, two more hours and I can go back home. I can breathe. I feel like I have more than paid my dues by now.

At least the boys will be here soon. *Boys!* I smile to myself. They stopped being that years ago. They're grown men now, with their own families, their own lives. But despite the fancy suits and manicured beards, all I see are two little kids who used to show up from school with scraped knees and elbows and spend hours fighting imaginary dragons and monsters. How I miss them.

I can understand that it must be hard for them to take the time every day to come by the hospital, but they do their best to visit, even if it's for a little while. Come sevenish they appear, and take it in turns to sit with their father. We're not allowed to be in the room all at once, so I chat with one or the other in the waiting area. Sometimes we talk about the weather, and at other times a little about their work. I usually ask for an update on the grandchildren whom I haven't seen since before the accident. Most days they ask me if I need anything for the house or if my back is giving me trouble, and then they leave. It has become a little ritual we go through, but it's one that I look forward to.

At least the two of us seem to have done something right.

All of a sudden, the machines start going mad. I see his large frame shaking uncontrollably and I shout for the nurse. They are already in the room – the beeping and screeching of the machines have them running to the bed.

Somebody gently pushes me out of the way and into the corridor. They are yelling things at each other, but I don't know what they're saying. I see the doctor, and he enters the room without even looking at me. I've seen him around the ward. He has a nice bedside manner – at least, nicer than the doctor who was here last weekend. This one reminds me of an ageing cherub.

The door closes behind him, and I can no longer hear what's happening inside.

I sit down on the chair outside and put my head in my hands. They're trembling. My breath is fast and uneven. I am ashamed of the feeling that is bubbling inside me:

Relief.

It rises from the depths of my being and threatens to engulf me. I want to laugh out loud, but I stop myself. After all these years I am about to be set free. Finally, we can both be at peace. He can be rid of the tubes and machines that keep him tied to this world and I can be rid of the chains that bind me to this life devoid of love, passion – even compassion.

I feel a hand on my shoulder, and I look up to see one of the nurses standing next to me.

'Is he…?' I begin.

The nurse shakes her head and says they are doing their best. She asks me if I would like some water or a cup of tea. I realise that my throat is dry and nod. Water would be lovely. She tells me she will be back in a jiffy. *Jiffy* – I wonder where the word even comes from.

I watch her as she hurries off – she's an attractive young woman with a trim figure and has a head of almost-jet-black hair tied into a ponytail swinging jauntily behind her. My husband would have approved. The same sweet words and cheeky smile that I fell so hard for were bestowed on any passable-looking female that crossed his path.

I have asked myself over and over again why I stayed, and the answer has always been the same. Whatever he is, he has always been a good father. We both love the boys, and however we might have felt about each other we wanted to give them a stable home. I think we tolerated each other at best. Somewhere in my mind I felt I was doing the right thing by keeping the family together.

A long time ago I tried to tell him that I wanted to leave, that things weren't working out. He didn't shout at me or even raise his voice, but he told me he would never let me take the children away from him. There was a coldness in him I had never seen before, and it was frightening. No one in his family had been divorced and we were not going to be the first.

I think I convinced myself that somewhere deep down he still loved me and this was his way of getting me to stay. I knew it wasn't true, but I never brought it up again.

I became immune to the late nights and the smell of perfume on his shirts, but it was the way he flaunted it that I found hard to swallow. That and the way he found pleasure in putting me down at every conceivable opportunity. I was his verbal punching bag. But he made sure he never said anything in front of the children. We had an image to maintain.

So I stayed for the sake of my sons, and when they were older I just accepted that this was my lot.

I have always looked with envy at couples holding hands, laughing with one another as they walk past in the street. I see them exchanging a quick embrace, a passionate kiss, and I wonder how it must feel to be loved and cherished. Maybe now I can.

The nurse is back and she offers me a plastic cup filled to the brim with water. I spill some on my hand when I take it from her. The water is cold and refreshing, and I gulp it down in one go.

The doctor comes out of the room and looks around. He sees me and I stand up, my legs feel wobbly. The verdict is about to be given.

He takes my hand and smiles at me. 'We've managed to stabilise your husband for the time being, but we will have to monitor him closely for the next twenty-four hours – I'm afraid he's not out of the woods yet.'

I slump back in the chair and the tears start rolling down my cheeks. They think I am overcome with relief. The nurse kneels down next to me and strokes my back. 'There, there, it's all right now,' she says in her soft calming voice.

I wipe my face and stand up. The nurse offers to walk me to the room. Right now I just want to be alone.

There are two other nurses fixing the sheets on the bed, so I wait by the door while they finish. They usher me in and smile at me as they leave. I try to smile back.

I walk towards the bed. He is lying there at the mercy of the machines around him. His face is obscured by the tubes.

I get down on the floor on all fours and look under the bed. The book has been kicked further under, so I reach across and retrieve it. I hold the side of the bed and stand up. The chair has been moved to one side and I drag it back to his bedside.

I want him to open his eyes one more time and look at me, to see that I am still here. I want him to know that when he's gone I'm going to be just fine. It's a waiting game now, and I have all the time in the world.

I sit down and make myself comfortable. It's dark outside, but the lights from the other buildings are twinkling. I open the book and find the page I was on and start reading silently. The boys should be here soon.

THE DESCENT

The faint scent of incense wafted through the shop from one of the back rooms. Maya pulled off her woollen gloves and stuffed them into the pocket of her black puffer jacket. The aptly named Geeta's Corner was warm and dry – a sanctuary from the blistering cold outside. It was surprisingly empty for a Friday evening.

The gregarious Mrs Sharma, or Geeta Auntie, as she preferred to be called, felt it made the shop cosier – or at least, more like her home. 'Last Christmas' was playing softly in the background. The incense was unusual enough, but the combination of incense and Wham was surreal.

'Hi, Mr Sharma,' she greeted the wiry gentleman behind the counter and smiled at him. 'A packet of Marlboro Lights, please,' she said, pointing to the shelf next to him.

'Maya!' A frown marred his lined forehead. 'You know you really shouldn't be smoking, dear, especially with your asthma.'

The concern in his eyes made Maya unable to meet his gaze. 'I know, I know,' she said. 'I'm trying to quit. It's much harder than I thought.'

145

'You've been saying that for the last six months! Geeta would kill me if she knew I was selling you cigarettes,' said Mr Sharma, shaking his head.

'Don't tell her, then,' Maya said, looking at him cheekily, a guilty smile playing on her lips. 'I promise I'll quit.'

He wagged his finger at her with mock admonishment. 'I'm not selling you any more after today, young lady.'

'Things are just hard around this time of the year,' she said quietly, a familiar constriction gripping her chest.

'It *will* get better – have faith, dear.' He gave her hand a pat as she passed him the money.

Two years and nothing had changed. Most of the time she felt numb inside. Time was not the healer it was meant to be. Her heart had long since shrivelled, serving no other purpose than to remind her she was still alive.

Mr Sharma handed her the packet of cigarettes and her change.

She deposited the coins into her wallet and put it back into her bag. 'Please give my best to Geeta Auntie, and don't tell her about my ciggies.'

'My lips are sealed – but not for long,' he said, winking at her. 'Hurry on home. You don't want to be outside in the dark, especially if it's going to snow heavily again. Well, that's what the weather forecast says, but who knows.'

Maya smiled at the old man. His simple gesture of concern made her eyes blur with tears. She waved to him and walked out of the shop before he noticed she was crying. She wiped her face with the back of her hand. Strange, she thought, how pity made her angry, but concern made her cry.

From the moment Maya and Yusuf had walked into Geeta's Corner late one evening five years ago, the Sharmas had treated them like family – they were both always welcoming and friendly; not just with them, but with anyone who walked into their shop. In fact, so much so that they knew all their regular customers by name, and were somehow privy to information about the goings-on in everyone's lives. Yusuf used to joke that the Sharmas were in fact part of MI5, and not some kindly shop owners, which was obviously just their cover – no one could possess the in-depth knowledge of the local community they appeared to have.

The outside greeted her with an icy blast of air, its suddenness taking her breath away. Snowflakes floated down and fell gently on her hair, speckling her coat with white flecks, which were covering the already snow-filled street with a fresh layer. It reminded her of the icing on a cake.

In her haste to leave the store, Maya hadn't noticed the man standing outside smoking, until she walked straight into him. Her packet of cigarettes fell on to the pavement, landing by his scuffed brown boots. She bent down to pick them up.

'So sorry,' she said, 'I didn't see you.'

'No problem,' he said softly, beating her to the cigarettes and handing her the packet.

Pale icy blue eyes met hers. For a second she felt the familiar sense of revulsion and fear as she looked up at him. The muscles in her back tensed. She thought there was a fleeting expression of surprise on his face. She immediately felt guilty for allowing her feelings to have been so visible. She wondered whether a day would come where she would be able to gaze into a pair of blues eyes without being tormented by visions of Yusuf.

'Thanks very much,' said Maya, taking the packet from him.

This time he smiled at her, showing a set of uneven teeth.

The cold was making the tips of her fingers lose sensation, and it took her a few attempts before she succeeded in lighting up a cigarette. She had, in the span of two years, gone from being a diehard non-smoker to taking up smoking – and not only that, but she had also embraced the myth that a cigarette could calm her nerves and provide release for her pent-up feelings.

Her wounds had become emotional scabs, easily picked away by the sight of gurgling babies or happy couples walking past, hand in hand.

Her phone buzzed. She took it out of her pocket. It was a text message from Alice:

What're you up to? Nearly home. Want to grab a bite somewhere?

Maya texted her back while walking:

Having a night in. Don't feel like going out. Thanks anyway.

They had been best friends at University, living in the same halls of residence in their first year, then sharing a flat for the remaining two years. Despite different life choices taking them on different trajectories, they had always stayed in touch. After graduation, Alice had decided to travel around the world for a year before accepting a job at a pharmaceutical company – a sort of last hurrah before facing up to the challenges of the real world.

Despite wanting to accompany Alice, Maya had followed the wishes of her family and joined a small firm of lawyers, putting life on hold as she pursued her career. A few years later she had joined Akin & Cuthbridge, an international law firm, as one of their up-and-coming corporate lawyers.

Relationships had been fleeting and marriage had moved down her list of priorities. It had, therefore, come as a total surprise when she had met Yusuf and her well-ordered life had been thrown into chaos. Not only had she said yes to his proposal without hesitation, they had been married within the year.

Maya put the phone back in her pocket and finished her cigarette, stubbing it out on a wall before throwing it into a nearby bin. The light of the streetlamps reflected on the white expanse of freshly fallen snow gave it a slightly eerie, luminous glow. She turned the corner leading up to her house. The road was silent – no cars, no people. It was as if the whole world had fallen asleep and she was its sole inhabitant. The only sound was that of the snow crunching underfoot. She walked slowly, so as not to slip on the ice forming on the ground.

The sight of her once-cheerful blue front door greeted her with the tired smile of a weary old friend. It needed a fresh coat of paint. In fact, the whole house needed a little love and care. The house, their house, was filled with memories of Yusuf, but it was also a painful reminder that he was no longer there. His absence had created an emptiness in Maya's life which felt like an ever-growing abyss. There were days where she had barely been able to drag herself out of bed. The pain of loss became a physical ache in her chest – consuming her, suffocating her, drowning her. At other times the tears would flow unbidden and unchecked. Mostly tears of despair and anger. Anger that Yusuf was gone.

Her mother had come and stayed with her for a while, but her well-intentioned words of sympathy, the 'life goes on' talks and constant hovering had just made things worse. Her father had wanted her to sell the house and move to Bangladesh with them, but Maya had firmly declined. She needed to grieve, but on her own terms, not on a predetermined time frame.

Fate interceded once again when Maya was at her lowest point. Alice's friendship provided such familiarity and comfort to Maya that she opened up to her in a way she hadn't been able to with anyone, not even her family. It had seemed only natural for Alice to move into the house with Maya while looking for a place of her own. Her presence in the house had been a godsend.

'It's like having a live-in therapist,' Maya had jokingly told Alice, but she wasn't far off the mark. It was Alice and her endless patience and practicality that enabled her to feel like she could face the world again.

She looked for her keys in her handbag, but the fading light made it impossible for her to see them. The inside of the bag felt cavernous, and the keys stayed hidden. She thrust her hand in with a disregard for the contents and searched for the jagged metal objects. Success! She retrieved them with a sense of victory. Then the click of the mechanism as she twisted the key in the lock.

Before she had time to open the door Maya heard a sound. As she turned her head she saw a hooded figure behind her – it was the man with the pale blue eyes. She opened her mouth to scream, but his hand, rough and calloused against her lips, came down like a steel clamp and stifled the sound. She could smell stale beer and cigarettes on his breath and the cloying scent of cheap aftershave. He grabbed her around the waist and hoisted her up. The more she tried to resist the tighter he wound his arms around her, till she could barely breathe. The door was kicked open by a booted foot and he walked inside, still holding her. And in that moment of sheer terror came a flash of clarity – Maya knew where she had seen the man before.

* * *

Maya and Yusuf stepped out of the Royal Opera House into an unusually mild mid-December's night. The Christmas lights were twinkling and the street was full of Saturday night revellers.

'I have to admit I enjoyed that more than I thought,' Maya looked up at Yusuf. 'Do I look a little more sophisticated and cultured to you now I've been to my first opera?'

Yusuf stopped on the street and held her at arm's length. He looked at her face with an exaggerated seriousness. 'Absolutely, my dear Eliza Doolittle, and you can start calling me Professor 'Enry 'Iggins!' he said, laughing. She loved the way it made his eyes crinkle at the corners.

'I know *La bohème* isn't the most uplifting – especially for your first opera – but it was pretty good, wasn't it?' he looked at her questioningly.

'Yes, but let's not rush back to see another one too soon. Baby steps, OK?' said Maya.

'Heathen!'

Maya laughed and linked her arm around her husband's.

'Talking about baby steps, don't you think it's time we thought of starting a family?' he said. 'I really don't want to put it off much longer.' The levity had gone from his voice and he was looking at her intently.

'Do we have to discuss this now?' she said. 'I'm not sure I want to give up my career just yet. We still have time...'

She wished he hadn't brought up the 'baby' topic. It was one of the areas where they both disagreed. He wanted to start a family as soon as possible and she wanted to wait.

'Fine. We can continue this conversation another time – but soon,' he said.

They walked side by side, Yusuf gradually retreating into a thoughtful silence. She didn't want the evening to end on a discordant note. 'I love this part of London,' she said. 'It's always so full of life and energy. Don't you think there's a certain joie de vivre that's lacking where we live? We should have bought a small flat here, you know. I would sit at my window and people-watch.'

Yusuf looked at her and rolled his eyes. 'Good God, the opera and French in one evening! Talk about cultural overload.'

Maya pulled a face at him.

'Anyway,' he went on, 'I guarantee that within the month you'd be tearing your beautifully styled hair out. Try side-stepping binge drinkers' vomit and listening to cars and ambulances driving past your window every night at all hours – seriously, you'd be begging me to take you away somewhere quiet and peaceful. In other words, to our lovely home, which I am desperate to get back to right now.' He sounded more like himself.

'Shoot down my dreams, why don't you?' she said, her face breaking into a grin. 'You're probably right, anyway. Let's just take a cab – I'm too tired to get on the tube.'

'Yes, Ma'am,' he said, scouring the street for a cab. 'We'll have to stop off at the shop on the way to pick up some milk.'

After a few minutes, he finally managed to hail a taxi. Maya sat in the back with her head nestled on his shoulder. Home was here, in his arms.

He was staring out of the window, and she sneaked a look at his profile – the dark hair cut short at the sides, his straight nose and full, sensuous lips. He always joked that his aristocratic nose made up for his dark complexion, otherwise he would be mistaken for a Bangladeshi farmer. She wanted to reach up and trace the scar which ran down the left side of his temple – a memento from his childhood, where he had run into a glass cabinet. She had never imagined she could love someone so completely.

They sat in comfortable silence till they arrived at their destination. Yusuf jumped out of the cab and walked up to the door of the corner shop. The Sharmas were about to lock up, but they let him in. A few minutes later he appeared with a milk carton in hand and clambered back into the cab.

The taxi made its way to their house. Yusuf paid the fare, took her hand and walked her to the front door. He opened it with an exaggerated flourish and gestured for her to enter first. She curtsied and stepped over the threshold.

The corridor was dark, except for the light coming in from the front porch. He took her in his arms and kissed her, milk carton in hand. They were light butterfly touches of his lips on her forehead, her eyes, the hollow of her throat and

153

finally her lips. They manoeuvred around the console table and into the living room.

The next few moments were a blur to Maya. She suddenly caught sight of a silhouette as they entered, and it lunged at Yusuf. She saw and heard the sickening blow to the side of his head. Yusuf stumbled, the milk carton falling from his hand.

The man grabbed her, and in the next instant she was aware of a cold sharp steel blade grazing her neck. 'Don't try to be clever,' he said. 'You don't want anything to happen to this little lady.' He still had the knife in his hand, but had moved it away from her throat.

Maya's eyes had adjusted to the dimness of her surroundings and she could see Yusuf's chest rising and falling rapidly. 'Look, we don't want any trouble. Just take what you want and go,' she heard him say.

'Shut up,' he barked. She noticed he was short and thickset, and he wore a ski mask which obscured his face. He pushed Maya and Yusuf on to the sofa. 'Get down here now!' he shouted to someone.

Maya heard the sound of heavy footsteps overhead, probably in their bedroom. The only items of any significant value were her jewellery and their electronic devices. They rarely kept an excess of cash in the house. She noticed both their laptops and iPads had been shoved into a large bag.

The short man gestured to her hand. 'Gimme your rings and the watch.' She complied without a sound. 'You too,' he said, looking at Yusuf, who immediately handed over his watch and wedding ring.

The man from upstairs entered the room, carrying Maya's jewellery box and Yusuf's watch collection – a weakness

Yusuf had confessed to when they had first met. He was far taller than his companion.

'We've got a problem,' grunted the short man.

'I can see that,' said the man to his partner, depositing the contents of his hands into the bag. He walked up to the sofa. 'Check the drawers.'

The short one passed the knife to him and went over to check the side cabinet.

The tall man took Maya's face in his hands, tilting it up towards him. Reluctantly she looked up at him. He was also wearing a ski mask, and only his pale, icy-blue eyes were visible. They lingered on her mouth then slowly made their way down her body. She shivered in revulsion. She felt Yusuf tensing next to her.

He knelt down beside her while his hand started sliding up her legs and in between her thighs. 'You're a pretty little thing. Ever been with a white man?' His mouth was so close to her ear that Maya felt a wave of nausea engulfing her. 'I could teach you a thing or two.' She tried to push his hand away, but he just laughed.

'Get your fucking hands off my wife,' Yusuf said, his voice was thick with anger.

'What? You don't want me to do this?' the man said, tracing the curve of her breasts with the tip of the knife.

Yusuf suddenly stood up and lunged at him, like a man possessed.

Maya screamed. She struggled to stand up, but was pushed to the floor. She could see Yusuf trying to wrestle the knife from the blue-eyed man. Then there was the flash of a blade and Yusuf staggered backwards. This time he was holding his stomach, a red stain spreading across his white shirt. She screamed again as he fell to the floor. The man with the blue eyes just stood rooted to the spot.

'What the fuck have you done?' shouted the short one. His voice was angry but laced with fear. He grabbed the bag and pushed his partner out of the living room. There was the sound of the front door opening, then silence.

Maya took her coat off and tried to staunch the bleeding. She managed to get her phone from her coat pocket and call an ambulance, all the while pressing down on Yusuf's wound. At first his breath came in short, shallow gasps. Gradually they became slow and laboured.

'Stay with me,' she kept repeating, the panic rising when his eyes started to lose focus. He opened his mouth, lips moving as if trying to say something. Maya bent her head to catch the words, but his words were inaudible.

The flashing of blue lights outside the window indicated the ambulance had arrived. The two men must have left the front door open, as the paramedics entered the room, announcing themselves. One paramedic disentangled Yusuf from her arms. The rest was a haze – all she could remember was them lifting him gently on to a stretcher. He never made it to the hospital. He had lost too much blood, and he never regained consciousness.

The two men had melted into the night without ever being caught.

* * *

The blue-eyed man kicked the door open and barged into her house, Maya crushed against his body. She felt light-headed. His hand still covered her mouth and nose. The door slammed behind them and he manhandled her into the living room.

'Bumping into you must have been a sign. We've got unfinished business, you and me,' he said into her ear.

Even through her jacket she could feel one of his hands on her breast. His grip loosened slightly. Summoning every ounce of strength, she elbowed him in his side. The impact of the thrust took him by surprise and he staggered, winded. In that instant, she managed to wriggle free.

She ran towards the entrance hall, but he lunged and yanked her back by the hair, which sent her reeling. Her arms flailing, she fell backwards on to the floor, her head hitting the corner of the coffee table. There was a sharp, sudden, excruciating pain in the back of her head. She tried to sit up, but the room spun around and her vision blurred. Instinctively her hand shot to the wound. She could feel something warm spreading across the back of her head. It was blood.

Maya looked up as the blue-eyed man loomed over her, his feet planted on either side of her legs. Without thinking, she grabbed his ankles with both her hands and pulled as hard as she could. The next moment he came crashing down, like a felled tree, cracking his head sharply against the wooden floor. But no sooner was he down than he attempted to stand up, raising himself up on to one side. He shook his head, visibly dazed, trying to clear his vision.

Somehow Maya made it on to her knees. She twisted to her side, reached out and picked up the large wooden elephant she knew she would find on the coffee table. She hoisted herself up and staggered towards the man. Then she raised the statue above her head and brought it down with full force on his skull. He barely saw the blow coming. His arm moved too late. Wood hit bone. He lay motionless on the floor. She knelt beside him, looking down at his face.

Her head was filled with visions of Yusuf, lifeless and blood-soaked. For a moment, she was overwhelmed with an awareness of her unfulfilled dreams, unfulfillable dreams – of her life without Yusuf.

The man moved almost imperceptibly. Maya picked up the wooden elephant, now stained, sticky with blood, and brought it down again as hard as she could. The scream that escaped her was guttural. This time he lay still.

A sudden weariness came over her, and her body gave way as she sank back to the floor. Her heart was racing and her breath was coming short and fast. She just needed to rest for a while. She heard the front door opening and closing, but despite trying to call for help, no sound emerged.

Alice was in the room sitting by her side, talking to someone on the phone, her face pale. She took Maya's hand in her own and said something, but everything felt distant and muffled.

'Ambulance on its way… you're going to be fine,' she thought she heard her friend say, but she could barely keep her eyes open. When she finally managed to look up, Yusuf was there, smiling at her. She smiled back and let the darkness engulf her.

THE CONNOISSEUR

The man in the ill-fitting brown suit at the adjacent table was talking in a voice meant to carry. 'Disgraceful!' he said, while trying to gauge the extent of his audience. Shamim looked up from his food, as did others at his own table.

'This biriyani is disgraceful. Where are the potatoes? Is there a shortage of potatoes in Bangladesh? And I tell you,' he said, pausing for dramatic effect, 'this,' and he pointed to the platter in the centre, 'wasn't made with ghee.'

A harassed-looking young man hovering nearby came running. 'No, no, uncle, I assure you we used ghee. Let me get you more potatoes.' His eyes darted to the guests seated around the other tables to see if they were listening. He was obviously a member of the bride's family, given his deferential demeanour.

'*More* potatoes? Ha!' His eyes were round with exaggerated incredulity. 'There wasn't even one!'

The uncle, who Shamim inferred was a guest from the groom's side, looked to his companions for affirmation. Some bobbed their heads in agreement; others looked away in embarrassment or gave their attention to the much-maligned biriyani.

The young man clicked his fingers to a bearer holding a jug of water in one hand and a few precariously balanced empty plates in the other. 'Hey, you, go and get a dish of hot biriyani. Make sure it has lots of potatoes. Go. What are you waiting for?'

The bearer nodded and scurried off in the general direction of the kitchens.

Shamim witnessed the scene unfolding and shook his head as he took a mouthful of said biriyani. He hoped his vociferous neighbour would pipe down before any more attention was directed towards him. He was used to being party to some form of drama at weddings – not all the weddings he had been to, but enough of them to make him relatively untroubled by it. If it wasn't the food – not enough potatoes in this case – it was the bride fainting during the ceremony due to the heat, the groom's party arriving late, hostilities ensuing because the bridal party was not adequately obsequious. It added a little spice to the festivities, but this loudmouth was too close for comfort. The sooner Shamim could eat and go the better. He chased the last few grains of the polao around the plate before scooping them up in his spoon. He would have used his fingers – it was inherently more satisfying than using metal utensils – but given everyone else was using forks and spoons he resisted the temptation.

The man next to him, sporting an impressive handlebar moustache underlining a bulbous nose, leant in. 'Can I pass you something? More biriyani? Some salad?'

'No, no, thank you, *bhai*. I'm full. Leaving space for the *mishti*,' Shamim said, patting his stomach and wondering what had engendered this sudden show of consideration.

They had barely exchanged more than the obligatory greeting since they had taken their places at the table. The attention was unwelcome. His eyes followed the man's gaze as he glanced over his shoulder to the table with the disgruntled guest. Shamim assumed the man thought he was part of the groom's entourage. To his relief, and that of his companion, the man in the brown suit was tucking into a plate of biriyani with gusto, temporarily appeased by the pile of potatoes heaped on his plate.

Shamim was sitting with a group of the bride's relatives. He gleaned this information from their few attempts at conversation, asking each other about some mutual relation or their respective health. They were quite the motley assortment. Opposite him was a middle-aged couple, who said nothing but ate enough food to put Shamim's appetite to shame. There was the moustachioed man and his wife, who disconcerted him somewhat by smiling benignly at him throughout the evening. There were two young women, the daughters of the middle-aged couple, who giggled more than they ate. Both were wearing brightly coloured, matching saris, one emerald green embellished with gold, the other a vibrant turquoise and gold, with a dazzling glut of sequins. Shamim's two-year stint working at a sari shop, amongst other jobs, gave him the ability to identify both the type, quality and price of a sari. He pegged them as good-quality, mid-range georgette. Every now and then the duo would whisper something to one another and peek at him under their long lashes, and he couldn't help gazing at them in admiration. He did, however, make sure that their parents were giving the food their undivided attention when he smiled back at them, not wishing to incur their disapproval. Next to the middle-aged man was someone who looked familiar. The slicked-back hair, the black-rimmed glasses. He couldn't quite place him. It would come to him when he wasn't trying so hard to think about it.

His eyes scoured the hall to see if dessert was imminent. The army of waiting staff were otherwise engaged, ferrying platters, jugs and plates through the maze of tables.

The Jasmine Wedding Convention Centre was abuzz with the sound of gentle conversation. A new structure in the Dhaka skyline, it boasted three different halls of varying sizes. Shamim viewed the vast hall with approval – it was the largest of the three and his favourite. It could accommodate most guests in one sitting, unlike some of the other venues, where you had to eat in batches. The raised dais at the far end of the room was bedecked in flowers, weighed down by the assortment of multicoloured blooms, much like the diminutive bride with the multiple necklaces hanging from her neck. The value of the jewellery on her person alone would be enough to set Shamim up for life.

He picked up his glass of borhani, taking a sip of the thick greenish liquid. As a child he had found the spicy yoghurt drink distasteful, and wondered why anyone would choose to drink it. But over time he had acquired a taste for it – even the pungent smell of the Himalayan black salt, or *bit lobon*. These days biriyani without a glass of borhani felt incomplete, and it helped him digest the rich food. Recently he had attended weddings where people had served fizzy drinks with the food. Just the thought of it made him baulk.

Two bearers clad in their white uniforms and turbans arrived in due course with trays, and placed the small clay pots of firni on the table. The first mouthful was an explosion of flavours. Shamim closed his eyes in reverence. It was exceptionally good. He used his spoon to scrape every last bit of the saffron-infused rice pudding into his mouth. He could have eaten a couple more, but there didn't appear to be any extras.

His belly was full, but it had not been a satisfactory evening. The uncle had been right – the biriyani must have been made with oil, or the ghee was of an inferior quality, and there was a distinct lack of potatoes. Biriyani without potatoes was sacrilege. Shamim had become quite the connoisseur over the years.

He thought of Haji *shaheb*, who would have raised his hands heavenwards in despair had he been alive. As a child, Shamim had lived down the road from Kachchi Biriyani Ghor in Old Town Dhaka, considered the best in the city, with people coming from all over. The goat meat would fall off the bones and melt in your mouth, while the rice was fragrant with ghee and saffron. The potatoes were always piping hot and buttery. Despite his ever-growing reputation and the demand for his food, Haji *shaheb* only ever made two large pots of biriyani a day, and when they were finished he closed shop. He didn't do it for the money, he would say. People were forgetting their roots and their cuisine, with all the new restaurants sprouting everywhere in the city serving Chinese, Thai, Italian, Korean and what not. Even biriyani was being bastardised, he used to lament.

'I'm so sorry, but I don't recognise you,' the middle-aged man said, as he pushed away his own empty bowl. 'Age is making my memory weak. Are you from Jalil's side?'

Shamim looked across at the man, at the strands of hair combed over his balding pate. It was a polite way of querying Shamim's presence at the table.

'Yes, I'm his second cousin from his mother's side of the family,' he said. 'Shamim.' He placed his right hand over his heart, tipping his head in a show of respect. The whole table was now looking at him with interest.

'I'm Farah's uncle, Asadur Rahman. And you are…?' This was directed at the man with the black-rimmed glasses. 'Also from Jalil's side?'

'*Ji*,' he nodded.

Not a man of many words, thought Shamim.

'*Achcha*, so you two must be related?' This came from the moustachioed man's wife.

Shamim and the man with the glasses exchanged a glance. 'I'm Jalil's cousin, but from his father's side of the family,' he answered.

'Very nice to make your acquaintance,' the moustachioed man said. 'I am Belal, and this is my wife Fatima. We are neighbours of Faruk *bhai* and Seema *bhabi*. Wonderful news about Jalil. We just heard from Faruk *bhai*.'

There was silence from both Shamim and Jalil's cousin.

'Yes, indeed,' said Shamim, feeling the perspiration forming on his upper lip as he spoke. 'We were all very happy to hear it too.'

'Farah is such a lucky girl. I've known her since she was this big,' the wife said, placing her hand level with the height of the table. 'Did Jalil say how long it might take to sort out the formalities?' Her large eyes were agog with curiosity. To his frustration, the bespectacled man stayed quiet.

'I don't know, but hopefully not too long,' Shamim said. A stab in the dark. This would be a prudent time to leave – it was fast becoming an interrogation. He debated how best to extricate himself from the conversation.

'It was a pleasure to meet you all,' said the man with the glasses, as if reading his mind. 'I'll take my leave, if you don't mind. Very early start tomorrow.' He pushed his chair back and stood up. His lips creased into a smile.

Shamim almost recoiled at the sight of his teeth crammed together, jostling for space within the confines of his mouth. Was it possible to possess more than thirty-two teeth?

'Yes, I should be leaving as well,' Shamim said, his chair scraping the floor as he arose. The girls seemed piqued at his sudden announcement, their smiles receding. He would have liked to stay a little longer and play the cat-and-mouse game with them, since it wasn't often he received attention from girls as pretty as these two. At the sari shop, the women barely registered his presence, let alone looked at him as a man – unsurprising, as he spent most of his time with a sari draped over his shoulder trying to convince potential customers to purchase Rajshahi silks, katans, Dhakai Jamdanis, georgettes or whatever fabric he was displaying. He was still, to his mother's disappointment, unmarried at the age of twenty-three.

Shamim raised his hand to bid them all goodbye, and strolled with studied nonchalance towards the exit. He spotted a table on the far right of the hall where they were serving tea and coffee, and wondered whether he could make a detour and get himself a cup of masala tea. Coffee after biriyani would have Haji *shaheb* rolling in his grave.

Many moons ago, Haji *shaheb* had caught Shamim scavenging alongside the alley dogs, going through the boxes that had been thrown away behind his shop.

'What's your name?' he had asked in a gentle voice.

Shamim bristled. Pity? He didn't want other people's pity. 'Shamim.' He looked at Haji Shaheb defiantly. Hunger had no pride, and he felt no shame taking the discarded food.

'Wait here,' Haji *shaheb* said, and disappeared inside his small eatery. Shamim had waited obediently and with trepidation, expecting some form of punishment for trespassing on Haji *shaheb*'s property. Later he wondered what had made him stay rooted to the spot rather than running away. After a few long minutes the old man emerged from the doorway with a box in his hand.

'Take this and come back next Friday,' he said.

The smell wafting from the box had been like the smell of heaven.

Every week after that, until he died of typhoid years later, Haji *shaheb* had given Shamim a box of biriyani to take home to his mother and younger brother. He had taken Shamim under his wing and given him a weekend job at his restaurant serving customers, though it had come with the condition that Shamim continue his schooling on the other days. This kindness Shamim had never forgotten — nor the taste of proper biriyani.

Haji *shaheb*'s face was as clear to him now as if he were standing before him. He could visualise his white cotton pyjama and white kurta, the tunic grazing the top of his knees, the embroidered cap he wore on his head and his beard which Shamim had watched turn from grey to white. After his death, his sons had taken over and expanded the shop. They had even opened one in Gulshan, where the elite of Dhaka society resided. They started cutting corners, using inferior cuts of meat and adulterated ghee, letting Shamim go when he had voiced his concerns. He wondered what Haji *shaheb* would have made of that. Now, opening his own biriyani shop was Shamim's dream, and an homage to his mentor.

Except for the firni, the food tonight had been disappointing. Despite wanting to finish the evening with a hot cup of sweet tea, he decided it was wiser to depart before being caught. He smiled at guests as he neared the doorway, waving his goodbyes to random people. Some raised their hands in response, but most had blank, confused looks on their faces.

He stepped into a blanket of humidity as he emerged from the cool air conditioning of the hall. The man with the glasses was standing by the gate next to the security guard, who was stretching his arms as a yawn ambushed him. Shamim stopped a few paces behind, in case the man engaged him in conversation and questioned him about the groom or his family.

'*Bhai*, is there a wedding here tomorrow?' Shamim heard him ask.

The guard nodded. 'There are three tomorrow evening, sir.'

'Till tomorrow, then,' he said, patting the guard on the back.

Shamim smiled. He knew where he had seen the man before. They had both been present at two other weddings

– one in this hall and the other at a venue two roads away. A fellow wedding crasher.

He made a mental note to stay away from the venue for the next few days in case their paths crossed again. He just hoped the biriyani next time would be better than Jalil and Farah's, cooked with proper ghee and with an abundance of potatoes – the way Haji *shaheb* would have made it.

WHEN CROWS COME CALLING

A wave of nameless faces rose to the surface with Zara, an army of human moles scurrying through the belly of London in its underground tunnels. Zara emerged into the sunlight and scrunched her eyes, momentarily blinded by the sudden brightness.

When she had first arrived as a fresh faced eighteen-year-old, using public transport was exciting. Exploring the city and discovering the fastest or easiest way to get around had seemed like an adventure. It had given her a sense of freedom and a feeling of independence she lacked in Bangladesh. Back home she lived under the watchful eye of society – much like living in a fishbowl. Privacy was an alien concept. Coming from a prominent family had its drawbacks, and the anonymity London offered her was liberating.

After three years the novelty had succumbed to repetition, and she had become another impassive statistic in the sea of commuters.

She rummaged in her backpack and retrieved a Walkman, which was in desperate need of replacement – held together by a rubber band. A flutter overhead made her pause and look up. A bird, its black feathers glistening in the sunlight like

169

oil-slicked hair, flew past and settled on a window ledge above a shop next to the station. The sight made the hairs on her arms stand on end. She still hated crows.

* * *

Dhaka was known as the City of Mosques, but the City of Crows would also be an apt title. The thought crossed Zara's mind as she and twenty-nine other thirteen-year-old girls watched in silent horror as a crow flew in through the open window of the classroom and, like a kamikaze pilot, headed straight for the fan at the front of the room. There was a loud metallic thud as it hit the blunt blades, flinging the bird as if on a slingshot across the room – feathers flying. All thirty pupils screamed in unison, jumped out of their seats and ran outside on to the veranda. The stragglers were still shrieking as crow feathers fell on their hair and clothes as they ran from the room.

Mrs Azim, the geography teacher, a short, squat, crotchety old woman, who saw it as her God-given duty to inculcate in Zara the necessity of the subject, was last to vacate the classroom. Instructions were shouted out to the girls to stand in twos, form a line and keep quiet. Mrs Azim hurried as best as her rotund frame allowed to fetch the caretaker Abul *bhai* to clean up the mess.

The commotion caused some of the teachers of the adjacent classrooms to venture on to the veranda and ask what was going on.

'Dead crow, miss. Hit the fan,' shouted one of the girls. With a nod or shake of their heads, the teachers disappeared back into their various rooms as if bird suicides disrupting lessons were a regular occurrence.

While they waited on the veranda overlooking the open courtyard of the school, some of the girls peered through the classroom window to view the remains of the crow, now resting on the floor. Zara's morbid curiosity caused her to look. It was surprising how little blood there was. They had dissected a frog in her biology lesson and she hadn't found it 'disgusting' like most of her peers – she wasn't particularly squeamish.

The bird had unknowingly martyred itself to halt what had been a particularly dreary lesson, and Zara sent a silent prayer of thanks heavenwards. Geography was the bane of her life. She certainly didn't care where exactly on the map of Bangladesh each of the rivers and their tributaries were situated. Nor were deltaic plains, tectonic plates or the population of various countries of any interest to her.

'You know when crows start cawing outside your window it's an omen that... someone's going to die,' said Maya in a theatrical whisper, pushing up her glasses back on to the bridge of her nose.

'If you whistle indoors at night snakes come and bite you,' offered Naila, whose love of embellishment was a source of amusement to Zara and her friends.

'I've heard that too,' Lamia said, her head bobbing up and down in agreement, eyes even wider than usual. Lamia would agree with anything Naila said.

'A crow dying like that,' Maya gestured to the classroom, 'must mean something really bad, don't you think?' She shuddered visibly, not wishing to be outdone by Naila.

'*Uff!* That's just rubbish,' said Zara, rolling her eyes. She had no time for superstitions. One less crow in the world wasn't such a bad thing. You were either being attacked by bird droppings during breaktime, if you were in the playground under the Krishnachura tree, or having your tiffin snatched straight out of your hands.

Zara felt a tug on her plait and looked behind.

'Hey, what did you get on the maths test?' Nisha asked, leaning forward from two rows behind, unaware of the conversation she was interrupting.

'Full marks,' Zara replied, a self-satisfied smile playing on her lips, though the credit was due to her father. If he hadn't come on to the veranda when she had been struggling with her algebra the result might have been very different.

He had strolled in and peered over her shoulder as she crossed out her workings for the tenth time.

'Baba, I *can't* do this equation. Help me!' she begged.

'"Can't" is with an 'aa' – not *can't*,' he said. 'I knew I should have put you in the British School, instead of listening to your Ma and sending you to a school run by American nuns. *Can't!* Uff! At least they teach British English at the British School.'

'Baba!' She was having a crisis, and all he could think of was correcting her accent.

He sat down on the rattan sofa beside her and took the pen from her hand.

'Most of my friends have an American accent,' she said. 'Why does it even matter?'

'Trust me, it makes a difference. You'll fit in better when you go to England for your law degree.' It was a statement that didn't invite any discussion and failed to acknowledge the possibility that she might have an independent thought on the matter.

Baba was a Supreme Court Judge, as his father had been, and was proud of his illustrious career and academic background. He took it for granted that she would follow in his footsteps.

Zara didn't have the nerve to tell him she had no desire to study in a stuffy old university in England. Much like her friends, she had been seduced by the freedom America seemed to offer – the land of *Knight Rider*, McDonalds and root beer. Not that she knew what root beer was, given that her knowledge was solely based on television programmes and films. But it sounded deliciously rebellious.

Her mother floated in, draped in a green cotton sari, with Jamila following behind her, carrying a tray of piping hot samosas and tea.

'What if I don't want to fit in?' Zara had mumbled under her breath.

Bad idea. This triggered a five-minute monologue on 'individuality versus conformity', which only ended when Ma suggested Baba should stop lecturing.

'Zara can always go to university in Dhaka – at least we'll have her at home,' she said, putting a samosa on Baba's plate.

'No way, Ma!'

'Absolutely not!'

'OK, OK, don't bite my head off! We still have a few years to decide.' Ma raised her hands in surrender and laughed, her gold bangles glinting in the light. 'At least that's something you both agree on.'

'Anyway, there's no such thing as can't,' Baba said, returning to the subject in hand. 'All you need to do is try.'

He set to explaining to Zara how to resolve her maths problem. She was surprised at how simple the equations seemed once Baba had shown her how.

'Time and tide wait for no man,' he said, looking at his watch, and planted a kiss on her head before leaving to get ready for a dinner with his colleagues.

* * *

'What did you get—' Zara began, but never got to ask Nisha what her marks were as she heard her name being called out from the front.

'Zara Ahmed, please come here.' It was Tahera, one of the senior prefects from class ten. 'Sister Barbara wants to see you now.'

A small bubble of anxiety rose from the pit of Zara's stomach and made its way to her throat. Being called to the headmistress's office normally meant trouble. It was the disapproval rather than the punishment itself which she found upsetting.

During the few minutes it took to descend the two flights of mosaic stairs, Zara tried to think what her misdemeanour might have been – could it be for not handing in her history homework? Or for burping loudly in her physics class, echoed by Nisha, sending everyone into fits of laughter? She couldn't think of any other reason why she might have been summoned.

Sister Barbara frequently meted out to punishment to her pupils. She called it 'character building'. Detentions, which consisted of standing outside her room doing nothing for an hour, or writing out lines, were top of the list – though writing lines was not too much of a hardship for Zara, as she had figured out the quickest way to accomplish this with the least amount of effort. You had to write the words out in columns: first the column for the 'I's, then the 'will's, then the column for 'behave', then 'in', and finally 'class'. Detentions were just a waste of time.

Her feet seemed to get heavier with each step. She looked down at her shoes, relieved she had used the chalk to whiten them earlier in the day. Dirty shoes, long nails and untied hair got you into trouble.

Tahera smiled as she gently nudged Zara over the threshold into the office. The room was spacious yet sparse, housing a desk and chair, a few filing cabinets and a well-worn cane sofa, which was currently occupied by Sister Barbara. Next to her was Zara's Sabina *khala*, her mother's younger sister. They both got up as they spotted her entering the room.

Zara's fears were compounded by her aunt's sombre expression. Sister Barbara gestured for Zara to come closer, and put a hand on her shoulder. Sabina *khala* opened her mouth to say something, but Sister Barbara spoke first. 'I'm sorry to give you the news, Zara, but your father has died.'

Zara stared at the lined and weary face gazing down at her, hearing the words but not comprehending their meaning. Sabina *khala* enveloped her in a tight embrace.

How could Baba die? She had seen him at breakfast, reading the paper, as he always did, smoking his cigarette. He had said he would collect her from school on his way back from court, and had promised to take her to get an ice-cream.

And that was it – no preamble, no run-up to the statement that would change her life for ever, just 'Your father has died'. She waited in silence while Tahera brought her schoolbag from the classroom. She gave Zara's arm a quick squeeze as she passed it to her.

The drive to the hospital felt interminable. Sabina *khala* held her hand; Zara let her fingers rest limply in her aunt's, neither returning the pressure nor moving her hand away. She stared out of the window at all the people going about their business, a thin rivulet of tears rolling unchecked down her cheeks. Rickshaws with a kaleidoscope of colours and patterns decorating their hoods wove in and out of the lanes, the footpaths teemed with people, street hawkers waved their wares just outside her window – everything was the same as usual, but to her all the sights and sounds of Dhaka suddenly felt unfamiliar.

'He had a heart attack, Zara,' her aunt continued. 'He didn't... they said he didn't suffer.' Her voice cracked.

Zara's mind was a jumble of thoughts. How could Baba be gone? If a bullet couldn't kill him, how could he die from a heart attack? She thought of the scar on his back where the bullet had torn its way out. The first time Zara had noticed it, she had been curious about the pinkish, shiny patch on the inner side of his shoulder blade. It was smooth to the touch except around the uneven edges, reminding her of a paint splatter. All he said was that he had been shot during the war in '71. He had shown her where the bullet had entered his chest. It was small and round compared to his back. He didn't say anything else – in fact, he never talked about it, and she sensed that for once her questions would not be welcome. Ma said that Baba had been shot by a Pakistani soldier during the war, but he had managed to escape. It had missed his heart by a hair's breadth.

Her eight-year-old mind had not fully understood the meaning at the time, but it had been enough to make Zara feel that Baba was invincible. She still did.

The hospital loomed ahead – a giant concrete monstrosity. The closer they got to the entrance, the more she wanted Sabina *khala*'s driver to turn the car and speed away. Bile rose to her throat, making her feel nauseous.

The lift was crowded, the smell of sweat permeating her cramped surroundings, and she held her breath till the door opened. Sabina *khala* guided her down a corridor leading to a set of double doors, where they were confronted by a throng of people, mostly familiar faces, a few unknown to her. Some were still crying, others talking amongst themselves, all unsmiling. There was a sudden hush as Zara and her aunt walked past.

A few of her relatives came forward and gave her a hug and offered words of comfort, but both the embraces and condolences were unwelcome. All eyes were on her, looks of pity drawn on their faces.

They stopped in front of a door with Baba's name on it. Her feet suddenly grew roots, and she stood stock still, unable to go in.

'Rima's still with Adil. She won't leave the room,' someone whispered to her aunt, referring to Ma and Baba.

If Zara opened the door, it would make everything real. Final. Somewhere inside her there was hope that it wasn't true: Baba wasn't actually dead; he was unwell, and there had been a mistake. He was bulletproof. When she walked into the room he would be lying in bed, smiling. They would both laugh about the mix-up. She remembered Baba telling her about Schrodinger's cat: you didn't know until you opened the box. She didn't want to know, and she didn't want to go in.

* * *

The sound of a car honking brought Zara back to the present, reminding her she was standing in a street in London and not a cold hospital corridor in Dhaka. Ma had let her kiss Baba goodbye, and she had been surprised at how soft his hair was. Cold cheeks, soft hair. It had always stuck in her mind.

When the time had come for her to choose where to study, what to study, it had been an agonising decision. The battle largely waged internally. Most of her friends had stayed in Dhaka, though some had gone to India and others to the US. Nisha was studying architecture at MIT. Zara's conscience had told her to pursue a career in law – it was what Baba would have wished.

'I *can't*... can't let Baba down,' she had said to Ma. But Ma had insisted that he would want Zara to be happy and to follow her dream. She wasn't so sure.

He had always insisted that she come home afterwards and practice law in Bangladesh. She could still hear his voice saying, 'Good men and women fought and died for this country – the least you can do is come back and serve your people.'

After many sleepless nights and much soul-searching, she finally allowed her heart to dictate, and filled in her application for medical school. And here she was in London, on her way to becoming a doctor. It wasn't law, but at least it was England. The guilt had never left her, but she hoped that Baba would approve.

Zara put on her headphones, pressing the play button with gentle fingers, and checked the time. The watch was far too big for her narrow wrist. The leather strap was worn and the face had a light scratch in the middle, but Zara loved it. It had been Baba's and she had put it on the day he died, only taking it off when she showered or slept.

She glanced at the black-feathered bird. It wasn't a sign or an omen or harbinger of anything; seeing it meant nothing – a mantra she repeated to herself every time she came across one. It was just a crow.

STRANGER IN THE MIRROR

The photograph on the table showed a slender young woman in a blue floral shirt and jeans gazing up at the man next to her, a smile on her lips. The man was laughing, his head tilted back, arm resting on her shoulder. There was something intimate about the way she was looking at him. I felt like a voyeur, an intruder. The woman, my mother, looked carefree, vibrant and, most importantly, happy – an emotion I had seen only in bursts and flashes. I remembered a woman whose smile didn't quite reach her eyes, a sadness in them I had never quite understood. I placed the photo face down on the table and rubbed my temple. The image of the two of them was seared into my brain.

There was an inscription on the back written in a bold hand, though the ink had faded over time: 'Always yours, Adam'. The man in the picture wasn't my father. He was a curly-haired man with dark eyebrows over smiling, hazel eyes. If I hadn't gone into my parents' bedroom after the funeral, I would never have found the photograph. It had slipped from my hand, the back of the frame coming loose when it fell on the floor. The photograph had been tucked inside.

It was strange to think that more than six weeks had passed since the accident.

When I arrived at the hospital, the woman at the reception had directed me where to go. The doctor who spoke to me had the careworn face of someone who had seen too much pain and suffering. He informed me that a lorry had skidded on the motorway and ploughed into their car. My mother had been killed instantly by the impact and my father hadn't regained consciousness after the crash.

'I'm very sorry for your loss, Mr Rasheed…' The information had been imparted with just the right balance of sympathy and calm. It was clearly not the first time he had given this kind of speech. My legs buckled. The doctor steadied me and led me to a chair.

DOA. Dead on arrival. And with those three words I was an orphan. Arguably 'orphan' was a term that could no longer be applied to me – after a certain age you cease to be an orphan and become 'parentless' instead – but at the age of twenty-four, orphaned is exactly how I felt. Losing both parents at the same time was something I never imagined I would have to confront. Identifying them was a cold and impersonal process. The sight of their lifeless bodies is an image I will never be able to erase. For days I walked around in a fog, my brain numb.

I'm not sure I could have dealt with the situation if it wasn't for Zia *chacha*, my father's younger brother. As soon as he heard the news he packed his bags and his family into their battered but dependable Volkswagen Passat and drove down from Birmingham. My *dadi*, Dad's mother, had died when he was still in school, and my *dada* passed away a couple of years ago. Since then it had just been the two of them.

'Don't worry about a thing, Amer,' he said as he embraced me, patting me awkwardly on the back. Displays of physical affection made him uncomfortable, reminding me of Dad. 'I'll sort out the funeral and burial arrangements.'

I could only nod my thanks. At the time I didn't even stop to think how hard it was for him to have just lost his brother.

The *janazah* service, the prayers for the departed, took place at the local mosque; never having been particularly devout, I was at a loss as to what the formalities and rituals were. Neither of my parents had been particularly observant, either. I had only attended a couple of *janazah*s before, when friends of Mum and Dad died, but then I had just copied everyone else. I told Mum afterwards that it was a bit like playing Simon Says, only in this case it was the Imam Says. I remember her trying hard not to laugh, and telling me off half-heartedly for my irreverence.

I had abdicated responsibility without a moment's hesitation, and was ashamed of how relieved I had been to accept my uncle's offer of shouldering the burden. Saira *chachi*, his equally efficient wife, had taken charge of looking after all the people who came to pay their respects, and for a while the house had hummed with life.

The burial had taken place straight after the *janazah*. We gathered on a crisp autumn day, the sun bathing the mourners in its golden light as we put my parents to rest. The finality of the situation hit me only when we lowered Mum and Dad into their graves, their bodies wrapped in white cotton shrouds. With each fistful of soil I felt as though the air in my lungs was being squeezed out.

A horn blaring outside made me start. I don't know how long I had been sitting in the kitchen, immersed in my thoughts, chasing a carousel of unanswered questions. The sun had gone down. The only light in the room was borrowed from the street lamps. A still life in sepia, I thought, looking around the room. Everything was just as it had always been – the same old white plastic clock that Dad had picked up from Woolworths years ago hanging over the door; the limestone tiles chosen with care when they had renovated the house; the motley collection of mugs my mother had accumulated over the years. Frozen in time, immortalising the past.

My fingers traced the initials carved into the wooden kitchen table – a show of teenage rebellion. 'I didn't bring you up to be a vandal!' Dad used to say when I did something he didn't approve of. 'It's that bloody Pete from next door that's making you behave like this!' He would replace the word 'vandal' with 'lout', 'ingrate' or anything befitting my perceived misdemeanour.

Poor Pete, my neighbour and childhood friend, took an inordinate amount of flak. 'That's what mates do,' he would say, and add that my mum's cooking was reward enough for putting up with it. He was living on the Gold Coast now, a surfing instructor, with his Aussie girlfriend. We spoke briefly after he heard the news of my parents. I wish he was here; his pragmatic advice would have been welcome. But the photo didn't feel like a topic you could discuss over the phone.

I needed a caffeine boost. The cupboard held an impressive assortment of teas with a lonely jar of instant coffee hiding right at the back, like an afterthought. Both my parents had a penchant for tea. I took out a mug that said, 'Keep calm and drink tea'. It seemed appropriate. The fridge had been emptied, but there was a carton of milk lurking inside. I sniffed it and gagged. It came out in clumps as I poured it down the sink, a rancid smell filling the air.

The kitchen was silent except for the ticking of the clock. The silence was unfamiliar. I could still hear the echoes of my parents' raised voices, arguing about something, everything and nothing. Thrust and parry, they were experts at fencing with words. It was like watching the same show on loop, ending only when Dad slammed the door behind him and retreated into the living room to drink himself into oblivion. Mum would sit at the table, her face blotchy from crying. 'You're such a good son; I don't deserve you,' she would say, as I made her a cup of tea and waited for the tears to subside.

Later, I would find Dad asleep on the sofa, his glass lying on the floor beside him and a whisky bottle on the table. I lost count of the number of times I helped him upstairs, finally getting him into bed after taking his shoes off. Picking up the marital pieces was a burden my parents had thoughtlessly deposited on my teenage shoulders, and I had resented them for it.

University had been my escape, a route to freedom, and I gladly accepted the offer from Edinburgh, getting as far away as I could. I never moved back home. When a job in London beckoned, I jumped at the opportunity, but rented a small flat of my own. Mum said I didn't come home often enough, but somehow life just got in the way. Now they were both gone. All I was left with was a room full of ghosts. Right now I would have done anything to see their faces and hear their voices.

There were times in the past few weeks I had called the home phone, letting it ring till it went to the answering machine just to listen to the recorded message. I wondered whether I would ever get used to the pain that had taken up permanent residency inside my chest.

'Always yours, Adam.' I read the words out loud. I could feel the tension building in my shoulders. I picked up the photograph, walked into the hallway and switched on the light in the downstairs toilet.

I held up the photo and scrutinised it against the reflection in the mirror. The mouth and face shape were different – my face was longer and more angular, while the man in the photo had a wider face with a square jaw. But the deep-set hazel eyes were similar to my own, down to the straight brows hanging over them. And the hair was unruly, like mine. I had never paid any attention to how little I resembled my dad – so I had never wondered why. It's not something you think about. People said I looked like Mum: she was fair, like a lot of Sylhetis; I thought I had inherited my colouring from her. Dad was of medium build and height, with a rapidly receding hairline. His face was round and more heavily set. Towering over both my parents at six foot two, I just thought I had got lucky and missed out on their short genes.

When Lily first saw the photo, she scrutinised it. 'Crikey, who's that?' she asked. 'One of your relatives? He looks just like you!' The comment had somehow taken root in my mind.

The harsh sound of the doorbell was a much-needed reprieve from my thoughts. I took a deep breath and walked back into the hallway. There was only one person I was in the mood to see, so I was pleased to see Lily's smiling face as I opened the door. She hugged me, standing on her toes to kiss me. I enveloped her in my arms and buried my face in her long, dark hair, drinking in the sweet smell of her perfume.

'How're you feeling?' she asked.

I shook my head wordlessly as I released her and shut the door behind us.

The kitchen was dark, and she switched the lights on. It brought me back to the stark reality of the present, banishing the ghosts of the past.

'What's that awful smell?' She wrinkled her nose in distaste.

'Sorry, forgot to throw the milk away last time…' I trailed off.

The photograph was still in my hand, and she reached out and took it from me.

'Did you find anything else?' she asked.

'Haven't got around to it.' I didn't tell her I had been putting it off.

'Why don't we order some food, then start with the photos? You never know – we might find something,' said Lily, already reaching for her mobile phone.

I don't know what I had done to deserve Lily, but I was grateful for her presence in my life. We had met on a train going up to Newcastle, sitting next to each other, and started up a conversation. A year later and here we were. She was my lifeline, keeping me sane while my world slowly crumbled around me.

Once the pizzas had been eaten and the boxes cleared away, we went upstairs. Over the years the guest bedroom had served a dual-purpose, housing visitors and an assortment of books, albums and boxes of unidentified objects – in fact, anything that had no place in my parents' day-to-day life.

We sat on the floor, each of us with a pile of photo albums and loose photographs we had found stored in one of the boxes. It was a strange feeling, flipping through the pages, seeing Mum and Dad gazing back at me. I'm not sure what I expected to find, but I needed to do something.

We sat in silence as we sifted through the photos.

'Good God! Is this you?' asked Lily, holding up a picture of a young boy with a fake moustache and painted beard.

'I'd forgotten about that. I was one of the wise men in the school nativity play. Must have been five.'

My parents were kneeling beside me, their faces filled with pride. I remembered how pleased they had been with me for getting a 'starring role' in the play. I flicked through snapshots of sports days with Dad, playing on the beach in Spain, ice-creams in Brighton, Mum sitting in the kitchen, the sunlight catching her face as she smiled down at me; but none of the photographs elicited anything other than a deep sense of nostalgia. With each album and each photograph, memories that had been relegated to the deep recesses of my mind began to resurface.

'I don't think there's anything here,' I said, feeling weary and defeated.

Lily nodded in agreement.

'I'm trying to think when all this changed,' I said, pointing to the photographs. 'Do you think it was because of him?'

'I don't know. Maybe,' said Lily, wrapping her arms around me. 'He was probably just an ex-boyfriend.'

'I wonder why Mum hid the photo – why she never mentioned him. It's not like we didn't talk about stuff.'

Lily disentangled herself and started putting the albums and photographs back in their boxes. 'Look, it's getting late. We're seeing Katherine tomorrow. Hopefully she'll know something.'

I hoped she was right. I took her hand and led her to the room next door – my old bedroom. The *Star Wars* poster hung above my bed, my guitar still on its stand in the corner of the room. They had left it untouched.

Later I lay on the bed, Lily's head on my shoulder, looking up at the ceiling. The last thing I remember before sleep claimed me was the image of Mum and Adam smiling.

* * *

Lily and I sat on a small red sofa in Katherine's flat in north Harrow waiting for her to say something. Katherine was Mum's best friend from her days as a student, and the two had always been close. Katherine had been a constant throughout my life, her presence solid and reassuring. I watched her face intently for any sign of recognition or emotion.

She looked up from the photograph. 'Jesus, this is a blast from the past! I do remember him. God, this was way back... when your mum and I were still in uni. I've forgotten where Roxy met him, but they...' She stopped and stared at the mug of Earl Grey tea in her hands. She was one of the few people who called Mum 'Roxy', shortened from Roksana.

'They what?' I could feel my body tensing like a steel coil wound too tight. Lily reached out and squeezed my hand.

'They were inseparable, even though he was studying in UCL. No – hang on, it was King's College, I think. He'd come and spend time whenever he could. At one point they even talked about getting married.' The look on her face made me realise that the loss of my mother, her best friend, was not inconsiderable.

'So he was an old boyfriend?' I asked.

'What happened?' enquired Lily.

Katherine put her mug down. 'All I know is that during the summer holidays in our... second year, it must have been, she called me saying she was getting married to your dad after she graduated. I don't think she had a choice. Sorry to say this, but your grandad was a bloody tyrant!' There was a flash of anger in her eyes. 'They found out about Adam... and God forbid a love marriage. I think Adam took it really hard—'

'Mum just married Dad because she had to?' I cut in. 'They told me it was arranged – the families knew each other...'

'Your grandad wouldn't let her finish her studies unless she agreed to the marriage.'

'Crikey, he sounds hideous, Amer,' said Lily, raising her hands in the air.

I didn't disagree. The last time I had seen my *nana*, a few years back, I had to stop myself from telling him he was an ignorant, opinionated bigot – a living anachronism. Thank God he had moved back to Bangladesh when I was just a kid.

'All I know is that your mum and Adam stopped seeing each other after that,' said Katherine. 'Though she told me she did meet Adam again a few years later – but that's all I know.'

'Before I was born?'

Katherine nodded. So Mum had seen Adam while she was married to Dad. I sat down and ran my fingers through my hair. I tried to think back, searching for any significant signs of what might have happened. Had Dad started drinking because he found out about Mum and Adam, the ex-boyfriend – maybe an ex-lover... The thought was like a punch in the gut. Were my parents really ever happy together? I knew that it was an arranged marriage. Mum and her family lived in London, and Dad had grown up in Birmingham. Right after she had graduated, my grandfather had fixed her marriage with Dad. The families had known each other for years. Mum had let slip a long time ago that my grandfather didn't approve of the friends she had made at university. I wondered if she was referring to Adam. They both looked pretty young in the photograph. Where was he now? The more questions I asked myself, the less I realised I knew. My parents were becoming strangers to me.

'She honestly tried to make a go of it with your dad, but ultimately they just weren't the right fit,' said Katherine.

'Did you take the photo?' I asked.

'I can't remember. I might have.'

Obviously I was aware my parents had a past, but the thought I had been trying to bury surfaced again. 'Can I ask you a question?'

'Yes, of course,' she said.

'Do you see any similarities between... Adam and me?' I said, holding up the picture.

She looked at the picture and then at me. 'I… well… there might be, but… I mean, now you mention it…' her hands rested on her lap and she twirled her ring around her finger. I could see her struggling to accept that her best friend may have kept secrets from her for decades as well. Betrayal wasn't as exclusive as I had thought.

People lie. It's a fact of life, and no matter how we dress it up a lie by any other name is still a lie. Sometimes we pretend we're protecting a loved one, but if we're honest we do it mostly to protect ourselves. Occasionally silence is easier than confronting the truth. I guess my parents were no different.

'You know, it might not be what you're thinking, Amer. She never told me. I'm not saying you're wrong, I just don't know,' said Katherine, with a shake of her head.

'Right now this is all conjecture,' Lily added. 'You don't know the full story. Seriously, if I were to say you look like some movie star, it doesn't mean he's your brother or your father. All we're doing is jumping to a whole load of conclusions. It might—'

'I know,' I said, cutting her off. 'But what if it is true? Katherine said Mum met up with him after she was married to Dad.'

'You could do a DNA test…' Lily said, looking expectantly at me.

'What, you mean exhume their bodies and get a sample of hair or saliva? Yeah, sure, why not!'

'Toothbrush, hairbrush…' She trailed off as I turned to look at her.

'This isn't a fucking crime drama,' I snapped. I knew I was being unnecessarily harsh, but the words were out before I could stop myself.

Katherine smoothed her short blond hair as she stood up. 'Give me a sec – I had an address for him or his parents – can't remember which, but it's from years ago.'

'Look, sorry babe, I didn't…' I started, as Katherine left the room.

Lily raised her hand and stopped me before I could finish. She said nothing as we waited, and I was grateful for the silence. The noise in my head was deafening.

After about five minutes, Katherine came back with a black-and-white floral notebook in her hand. 'Thank God we used to actually write things down in our day,' she said, and sat back in the armchair opposite the sofa and flicked through the pages. 'Adam,' she said, a look of triumph on her face.

I felt as if the air had been sucked out of the room. For a moment it was hard to breathe. I took the diary from her and read. His name was Lucas Adam.

As if reading my mind, Lily said, 'Wonder why on earth he went by his last name?'

'Not sure, actually,' replied Katherine, her face creasing into a frown. 'We all called him Adam.'

'Thank you, Katherine, I really appreciate—'

'I wish I could do more. I wish I knew more. Amer, he probably doesn't live there any more, but I hope it's a start.'

I wondered how many Lucas Adams there were in the world. But at least I had a name and an address. It was definitely a start.

'So what do you want to do?' said Lily, pulling the cushion against her chest.

'I don't know,' I said, handing the diary back to Katherine. What I did know was finding Lucas Adam would be the only way to make sense of what the photo signified. Acknowledging that something might be true was one thing; knowing that it was true was another. But accepting the truth... I wasn't sure I could deal with that. At least, not for now.

THE SKIN YOU WEAR

The euphoria of the last few hours is rapidly fading, my irritation growing by the minute. Nausea and hunger chase each other, swinging from one to the other like a manic pendulum, which isn't helping my mood. What no one had told me was that the time of day in 'morning sickness' is a euphemism for 'all the time'.

The text from Azim has managed to burst the bubble of happiness that is insulating me from my discomfort.

Leaving the office now. Start ordering if you're hungry.

He's going to be late – again. It wouldn't have mattered as much if it had been any other day. I could have dealt with a meeting running over, or an unscheduled conference call, but it is a big day for both of us and now I have to wait.

I come out of the cubicle and take a few of the paper towels stacked on the counter, wiping my hands with more vigour than necessary. The 'OUT OF ORDER' sign stuck to the hand dryer is still there from my last visit, barely held in place by a flimsy strip of masking tape. The place is desperately in need of a bit of TLC. Fortunately, the service is friendly and the food consistently good. Levant is a gem of a restaurant we had discovered and fallen in love with since moving to the area.

There is a commotion from the interior of the restaurant – loud voices that make me roll my eyes. I assume it's a group of people from the nearby offices for a pre-Christmas dinner. They are always the noisiest. I hope their rowdiness won't detract from my enjoyment of the evening. Despite being situated on a slightly quieter road just off the main street, flanked by a florist and nail salon, the restaurant is a popular one.

I had been so lost in my thoughts on the way from the bus stop to Levant, I had almost walked straight past two of my sixth-form students. I only noticed them after they shouted a 'Hi miss' at me. In my defence, it's also often hard to recognise them when they are out of uniform and have a ton of make-up on. I return their greeting and wave as they cross to the other side of the road. The sound of their youthful voices and laughter floating in the air behind me makes me smile.

Living so close to the school makes bumping into my students an occupational hazard. It was a surprise to my family when I first announced my intention of becoming a teacher. My parents had hoped I would become a doctor. Baba was an oncologist, Ma a GP and my sister an orthopaedic consultant. I joked that we had all medical bases adequately covered.

Apart from the girls, there were hardly any people on the street – just a group of men standing outside the door of the restaurant when I arrived, heads together, conversing in hushed voices. I wondered as I passed why young people these days are always dressed in black funereal hoodies.

I delve into my Tardis-like handbag and retrieve the rose-scented hand cream lying at the bottom and squeeze a blob on my palm. It is part of a Christmas gift from my students. The envelope nestled in my bag between my wallet and a copy of *Julius Cesar* calls out to me. Just one more look. I take the photo out and place it on the mottled granite surface, but leave the accompanying DVD where it is. The image of the baby growing inside me is a source of wonder, but my excitement is tempered with caution. I don't want to jinx this. There have been too many false hopes and disappointments over the years. Having to deal with the looks of pity and sadness in other people's eyes compounded by my own sense of loss is emotionally draining.

I am far too intimately acquainted with the word 'barren' being used behind my back – as if my womb is a wasteland I have control over. Azim has reluctantly promised not to tell anyone, not even our families – at least, not until the first trimester is complete. It has been a feat of great self-restraint to stop himself from announcing the news to the world. Today I have finally crossed the three-month mark.

A little more rummaging is required before I find my lipstick.

My subconscious must have pre-empted Azim, and thankfully I had ordered some starters before his message flashed on my phone. Mr Khoury, the manager, laughed as he escorted me to a table towards the back of the room, knowing before I opened my mouth what I wanted. 'Shall I get you some bread and houmous with some olives, Mrs Aslam?' The olives were a given. 'And a fresh mint tea?'

'Yes, please,' I say before heading to the toilet. I was obviously far too regular a customer. I am looking forward to tucking into the dishes. I might get their shish taouk as my main – the chicken practically melts in your mouth.

These days there is a vast black hole where my stomach used to be, and I am continuously hungry. This is what Erysichthon, King of Thessaly must have felt like after the goddess Demeter cursed him with an insatiable hunger – though if I remember correctly he ultimately devoured himself. At least I have a miracle growing inside me to account for my voracious appetite.

The doctor I saw for my scan told me everything appeared to be 'AOK' – apparently people still say that. Once I show Azim the ultrasound scan we can finally break the good news. I place a hand on my stomach and wonder when people will start noticing my expanding belly and offer me a seat on buses or the underground. At three months my bump is barely visible, especially under my bulky coat. Maybe I can get one of those 'Baby on Board' badges.

After years of trying to conceive and undergoing numerous IVF treatments, we had been on the verge of giving up, even discussing the possibility of adopting, when the doctor announced I was pregnant. At the age of thirty-nine I am going to have a baby. I am going to be a mother. Dreams can actually become a reality. I insisted on donating money to a children's charity as a way of giving thanks for our unexpected blessing.

A noise that sounds like a firecracker makes me jump. The lipstick drops from my hand into the basin, leaving a pink smear on the white porcelain surface. There are screams. For a split second I think it is a gunshot, but dismiss the idea almost immediately. I have never heard one, except on TV. But then there is the noise of chairs scraping across the floor.

Against my better judgement I open the bathroom door and edge my way forward into the corridor that leads up to the main area of the restaurant. I can hear raised angry voices and people crying. It takes me a few seconds to realise that the loud thumping noise in my ears is my heart.

'Shut the fuck up!' someone yells. 'You, get over there.' The muscles in my body tense. It takes every ounce of willpower to peer through the small circular window in the door overlooking the restaurant. A man is standing in the middle of the room with his back to me, but I can see him holding something in his hand, which he waves around indiscriminately. It is a gun. My legs feel leaden – heavy and immobile, keeping me rooted to the spot. I stand still – not by choice but out of fear.

Another man is manhandling the kitchen staff into the room. The customers and waiting staff are huddled on the floor, some of them holding on to each other, their faces caricatures of themselves, contorted in terror and disbelief. At the far end of the room I see a man lying on the ground, a claret-coloured stain blotting his white shirt like he has spilt wine on himself. It is the motionless body of Mr Khoury.

I press my hand to my mouth to stifle the scream that threatens to escape and duck my head. A wave of nausea hits me and for an instant, I am unsteady on my feet. I retch but nothing comes up except bile. It burns my throat. It takes a few seconds before I can bring myself to look again. Another man is standing in front of the entrance to the restaurant, blocking the door. The Venetian blinds have been pulled down. It is only then that I notice the people are separated into two groups: white and non-white. The attackers do not attempt to hide their faces.

Part of me is transfixed by the unfolding horror scene on the other side of the window. It feels surreal. Almost as if he senses he is being watched, the man with the gun turns around and looks towards the door I am standing behind.

'Go check the bathrooms,' he says to the one nearest to him, who also has his back to me. I spin around and run back into the toilets. My bag is lying on the counter and I grab it, before locking myself in the stall furthest from the door. But as I fumble inside, my fingers searching frantically for my phone, I realise with a mounting sense of panic that it isn't there – I have left it in the pocket of my coat, which is still hanging over a chair in the restaurant.

I sit on the toilet seat and raise my feet, tucking my knees under my chin. It dawns on me that he is hardly going to look under the door to see if anyone is inside – the door being locked is a giveaway. I get up and stand in the corner of the small cubicle, wedging myself between the toilet and the narrow plastic bin, hugging the bag to my chest. My rational self tells me it makes no difference where I stand or sit, but fear overrides judgement. Those few additional centimetres from the door make me feel safer.

My breath catches in my throat as I hear the man shouting from the corridor. 'Found one of them hiding in the bathroom! Fucking coward.'

Whoever had been hiding in the men's toilet is pleading. 'Please… please… don't.' His voice breaks. I think I can hear the sound of a scuffle outside, followed by the same loud popping I have heard before. And then again. This time there can be no mistake – they are gunshots, followed by screams from the restaurant.

My legs buckle under me, and I sit down on the closed toilet seat and put my head in my hands. This can't be happening. I am oblivious to the tears that have started streaming down my cheeks until I see them falling like raindrops on my bag. I dash them away with my hand. My breath comes in short sharp gasps. It's like trying to breathe underwater.

I remember Azim telling me about an attack a couple of months ago in an Indian restaurant where four young men had walked in and killed three customers because they were 'foreign-looking'. According to the media, they were an organised group of far-right white supremacists. What was even more chilling was that they had then given themselves up without a fight when the police arrived, claiming they were purging the nation of filth. It had been on the news, and the papers carrying the story had reported a rise in the number of race-related violent hate crimes in and around London. Pigs' heads being left in front of mosques, a few arson attempts in a mosque and a synagogue, women having their hijabs ripped off, 'go home' painted on walls and doors of people from parts of Eastern Europe. There had also been a disturbing report of a group, whose name I can't remember, reviving and emulating the Hitler Youth of Nazi Germany. Growing up as a brown Muslim woman in England I have had my fair share of 'Paki' bandied at me, but I have never been as acutely aware of the colour of my skin as I am at this moment, sitting in a toilet cubicle.

I close my eyes, rocking my body back and forth, trying to remember the prayers I was made to recite as a child.

Azim isn't religious, and I have allowed myself to gradually drift from the faith I was born into. I can't concentrate – the more I try the more the verses elude me; it is like grasping at wisps of smoke. What if Azim arrives? He is bound to know something is wrong if the restaurant is closed. Right now I don't want him anywhere near. For once I am grateful he is late. The realisation that this was the group outside the restaurant dawns on me.

The door of the bathroom slams open and heavy footsteps stop outside my stall. The man pushes the door and, finding it locked, bangs on it. The flimsy barrier shakes with the force of his fist.

'Open the door!'

I sit on the toilet, unable to move, trying to hold my breath.

He thumps on the door again. 'Don't make me get you! Open the fucking door!'

Or I'll huff and I'll puff and blow the door down – the line appears in my head like an unwanted visitor. For a split second a bubble of hysterical laughter makes its way to my throat, where it dies. I stand up, my hand shaking as I unlock the door.

Brown eyes meet blue: fear in mine, anger smouldering in his.

Then there is a moment of recognition.

'Jason?' I ask. I stare at the young man in front of me. I had been his English teacher for two years and his form tutor for one. His once floppy, unkempt blond hair is cropped close to his skull. The school uniform has been replaced by black jeans, scuffed-up boots and a black hoodie.

'Shit, it's you,' he says. He has a gun in his hand and is pointing it at me. 'You gotta come with me. I wish you hadn't come here tonight,' he says, running his other hand over his shorn head.

For a brief moment I wonder if I can detect a hint of guilt or remorse in his voice. 'Please, you don't have to do this... I—' I start.

'Just stop talking!'

'Jason, I've known you since you were a kid.'

'Shut the fuck up. Who the fuck do you think you are? Fucking foreigner, teaching me my own language!' He reaches forward and grabs me by the wrist.

I'm not a foreigner, I want to say. I was born here, just like you. But I keep my mouth shut, and my attempt to pull out of his grasp is futile. His hand is like a vice as he drags me out of the cubicle.

'Please... please don't do this!' I beg, barely able to recognise my own voice. 'I'm pregnant.'

His hand loosens almost imperceptibly. 'You shouldn't have come here,' he repeats.

A glimmer of hope flickers in my heart. His face is out of focus as I look at him through the tears misting my eyes.

Then he turns his face away and pulls me along. The black-and-white image of the ultrasound of my unborn child is still lying on the countertop, next to the basin.

I look back as the door of the bathroom swings shut after us.

ACKNOWLEDGEMENTS

I am eternally grateful to my mother, Halima Kabir, who left us in 2021, for her unwavering love and encouragement, allowing me to forge my own path, and to my brother Junaed Kabir, who has always believed in me.

To my children, Ayesha, Mikhail and Iman, my staunchest supporters and harshest critics, thank you for sharing me with the characters in my stories. I love you beyond measure.

A special thanks to Laura Ferguson, Isabel Fernandes, Omar Mohsin and Farzeen Khan Chowdhury for always having faith in my writing and cheering me on, and Hissam Khandker, Shakeel Mowla, Trish Dhanak and Ismet Joseph for your support.

I am indebted to my long-standing editor and mentor, Aasha Mehreen Amin at *The Daily Star*, for encouraging my love of writing and giving me my first column.

I would like to express my gratitude to fellow writer, poet and friend Ahsan Akbar, for giving me the impetus to finish writing *Truth or Dare* in the first place, and to Bengal Lights Books for publishing my book.

Truth or Dare has been a labour of love and I cannot thank the wonderful Will Dady and Renard Press enough for breathing new life into the collection, and renewing my belief that dreams can come true.

Last but not least, I would like to thank my husband Roger for his patience in putting up with my endless procrastination and self-doubt, for reading every draft of every story and for being my sounding board. Without his love and support, none of this would have been possible.

NADIA KABIR BARB

DATES OF

FIRST PUBLICATION

'Let Me Go' first published in *The Missing Slate* in 2015

'Can You See Me' and 'The Descent' first published in *Eclectic Mix* (Volume Five) in 2016

'Inside the Birdcage' first published in *Open Road Review* in 2016

'The Lives of Others' first published in *The Missing Slate* in 2016

'Living with the Dead' first published in *Bengal Lights Journal* (8) in 2017

'Truth or Dare' first published in *Six Seasons Review* 2017/ *Wasafiri* in 2017

'Don't Shoot the Messenger', 'The Truth about Sam', 'Broken', 'In Case I Die', 'The Enlightenment of Rahim Baksh' and 'My Father's Daughter' first published in *Truth or Dare* in Bangladesh by Bengal Lights Books in 2017; 'Can You See Me', 'Inside the Birdcage', 'Truth or Dare', 'The

Lives of Others', 'Let Me Go' and 'The Descent' and also published in *Truth or Dare* in Bangladesh by Bengal Lights Books in 2017

'Living with the Dead' also published in *May We Borrow Your Country* by Linen Press in 2019

'The Connoisseur' and 'Stranger in the Mirror' first published in *Tongues and Bellies* by Linen Press in 2021

'When Crows Come Calling' first published in *Golden Bangladesh at 50* by The University Press Limited in 2021

'Over the Edge' and 'The Skin You Wear' first published in this volume in 2023

ABOUT THE AUTHOR

NADIA KABIR BARB is a British Bangladeshi writer and journalist. Her work has been published in international literary journals and anthologies including *Wasafiri*, *The Missing Slate*, *Open Road Review*, *Eclectic Mix*, *Golden Bangladesh at 50*, *Bengal Lights* and *Six Seasons Review*. She was longlisted for the 2021 Bridport Prize Peggy Chapman-Andrews First Novel Award for *Walk in My Shadow*. She has an MSc from the London School of Economics and the London School of Hygiene and Tropical Medicine, and has worked in the health and development sector in both the UK and Bangladesh. *Truth or Dare* is her debut collection of short stories. Nadia lives in London.